BESSIE HEAD

MARU

Heinemann

Heinemann Educational Publishers
A Division of Heinemann Publishers (Oxford) Ltd
Halley Court, Jordan Hill, Oxford OX2 8EJ

Heinemann: A Division of Reed Publishing (USA) Inc.
361 Hanover Street, Portsmouth, NH 03801-3912, USA

Heinemann Educational Books (Nigeria) Ltd
PMB 5205, Ibadan

Heinemann Publishers (Pty) Limited
PO Box 781940, Sandton 2146, Johannesburg, South Africa

OXFORD MELBOURNE AUCKLAND
JOHANNESBURG BLANTYRE GABORONE
IBADAN PORTSMOUTH (NH) USA CHICAGO

© Bessie Head 1971

First published by Victor Gollancz Ltd, 1971
First published in the African Writers Series in 1972
Reprinted seven times
Published in B Format in 1987
Reprinted eighteen times
First published in this edition in 1995

Series Editor: Abdulrazak Gurnah

British Library Cataloguing in Publication Data
A catalogue record for this book is available from the British Library.

ISBN 0 435 909630

Cover design by *Touchpaper*
Cover illustration by Jeff Fisher
Author photograph by George Hallett

Printed and bound by
Interpak Natal, Pietermaritzburg
95 96 97 98 99 8 7 6 5 4 3 2 1

BESSIE HEAD, one of Africa's best-known women writers, was born in South Africa in 1937, the result of an 'illicit' union between a black man and a white woman. Her life was a traumatic one, and she drew heavily upon her own experiences for her novels. She was looked after by a foster family until she was thirteen, and then attended a mission school. She trained as a teacher. After four years' teaching she took a job as a journalist for *Drum* magazine, but an unsuccessful marriage and her involvement in the trial of a friend led her to apply for a teaching post in Botswana, where she took up permanent exile. Her precarious refugee status lasted fifteen years until she was granted Botswana citizenship in 1979.

Botswana is the backdrop for all three of her novels. *When Rain Clouds Gather*, her first novel, based on her time as a refugee living at the Bamangwato Development Farm, was published in 1969. This was followed by *Maru* (1971) and the intense and powerful autobiographical work *A Question of Power* (1974). Her short stories appeared as *The Collector of Treasures* in 1977, and in 1981 *Serowe: Village of the Rain Wind* was published, a historical portrait of a hundred years of a community in Botswana.

Bessie Head died in 1986, aged 49. *A Woman Alone*, a collection of autobiographical writings, *Tales of Tenderness and Power* and *The Cardinals* were published posthumously.

Part One

The rains were so late that year. But throughout that hot, dry summer those black storm clouds clung in thick folds of brooding darkness along the low horizon. There seemed to be a secret in their activity, because each evening they broke the long, sullen silence of the day, and sent soft rumbles of thunder and flickering slicks of lightning across the empty sky. They were not promising rain. They were prisoners, pushed back, in trapped coils of boiling cloud.

Like one long accustomed to living in harmony with the earth, the man had continued to prepare his fields for the seasonal ploughing, and even two brand new water tanks had been fixed to the sides of his small new home to catch the storm water, when it rained. He wanted a flower garden of yellow daisies, because they were the only flowers which resembled the face of his wife and the sun of his love. If that were one of his preoccupations, there were a thousand others as well. Maybe life was too short. Maybe life had presented him with too many destinies but he knew that he would accept them all and fulfill them. Who else had been born with such clear, sharp eyes that cut through all pretence and sham? Who else was a born leader of men, yet at the same time acted out his own, strange inner perceptions, independent of the praise or blame of men?

'I'll be going home now,' he said quietly, to a group

of three men working on the construction of vegetable beds.

He had hesitated before speaking. The men were no ordinary farm workers, but close friends who had surrounded and protected him all his life. He added a word or two which made them shake their heads behind his back and mutter: 'Maru is always impossible!'

'Ranko,' he said sharply, pretending annoyance. 'Didn't I tell you not to break up the clods? They are for conserving moisture in the soil.'

Ranko looked up, raised one hand and rubbed the side of his nose. Sudden, sharp words and the mention of his name threw him into confusion. Ranko meant 'big nose' in Setswana, and when had people not had vegetable garden soil raked in a fancy way? Every new and unacceptable idea had to be put abruptly into practice, making no allowance for prejudice. It was painful, like his big nose, and who knew where life and destiny would take the three of them as long as their lives were attached to Maru? They began shaking their heads, and the gesture was very deep. The man who slowly walked away from them was a king in their society. A day had come when he had decided that he did not need any kingship other than the kind of wife everybody would loathe from the bottom of their hearts. He had planned for that loathing in secret; they had absorbed the shocks in secret. When everything was exposed, they had only one alternative: to keep their prejudice and pretend Maru had died. But did it end there? Was that not only a beginning?

Only Maru knew the answers. He paused awhile and looked towards the low horizon where the storm brooded.

The thorn trees turned black in the darkening light and a sudden breeze stirred the parched, white grass. There was so little to disturb his heart in his immediate environment. It was here where he could communicate freely with all the magic and beauty inside him. There had never been a time in his life when he had not thought a thought and felt it immediately bound to the deep centre of the earth, then bound back to his heart again – with a reply. Previously, the stillness with which he held himself together to hear the reply had always been disrupted by people. People were horrible to him because they imagined that their thoughts and deeds were concealed when he could see and hear everything, even their bloodstreams and the beating of their hearts. If they knew all that he knew, would they not have torn him to shreds some time ago, to keep the world the way it was where secrets and evil bore the same names? It was a vision of a new world that slowly allowed one dream to dominate his life.

A little brown, dusty footpath turned away from the roaring busy highways of life. Yellow daisies grew alongside the dusty footpath and danced in the sun and wind, and together the footpath and the daisies would make his heart bound with joy. As soon as the first rains fell he would plant those yellow daisies along the footpath leading to his home – so simply and precisely did he translate his dreams into reality. At least, the present was simple. But there was a depth of secret activity in him like that long, low line of black, boiling cloud. There was a clear blue sky in his mind that calmly awaited the storm in his heart and when all had been said and done, this earth would be washed clean of all the things he hated. He slowly continued his walk home, his gaze turned towards the horizon. It was very beautiful.

So quietly did he enter the house that his wife looked up fearfully from her work of preparing the table for the evening meal. He sometimes had vicious, malicious moods when every word was a sharp knife intended to grind and re-grind the same raw wound. Most certainly, no memory remained in her heart and mind of previous suffering. Most often she felt quite drunk and mad with happiness and it was not unusual for her to walk around for the whole day with an ecstatic smile on her face, because the days of malice and unhappiness were few and far over-balanced by the days of torrential expressions of love. Maybe a dark shadow had been created to balance the situation. Maybe some blot of human wrong had to happen to force Maru to identify himself with the many wrongs of mankind. He moved too swiftly and surely. He never doubted the voices of the gods in his heart. It was only over the matter of Moleka that he was completely undone, not the way one would expect a wrong-doer to be undone. He was thrown off-balance by the haunting fear that he would one day be forced to kill Moleka, one way or another.

There were two rooms. In one his wife totally loved him; in another, she totally loved Moleka. He watched over this other room, fearfully, in his dreams at night. It was always the same dream. Moleka would appear trailing a broken leg with blood streaming from a wound in his mouth and his heart. No one ever cried with such deep, heart-rending sobs as his wife did on these occasions. Often he would start awake to find those hot tears streaming on to his arm from her closed eyes.

'Why are you crying?' he'd ask, pretending not to know. But she would see the tears too, yet be unable to account for them on waking because she had no mental impression of her dreams, except those of the room in which she loved Maru. There was nothing he could invent to banish the other room. He seemed to be its helpless victim and it was not much to his liking as jealousy was almost an insanity in him and the inspirer of it was nearly his equal. No one else was. To Moleka he had made so many concessions, he did not care to make others. He had ensured that Moleka had the next best woman in the world. The next best woman in the world had more intellectual attainments than his wife. She had style and class and immediately impressed people as someone worth noticing and listening to. All these things flattered Moleka, as he was also a man who impressed people. What did he want with a woman who meant nothing to the public? In fact, until the time he married her she had lived like the mad dog of the village, with tin cans tied to her tail. Moleka would never have lived down the ridicule and malice and would in the end have destroyed her from embarrassment.

There was always the public. A man with a public eye tried to please them. Once he had decided to act, he had based his calculations on what was good for Moleka and what was good for him. He brooded over this. Perhaps he had seriously miscalculated Moleka's power, that Moleka possessed some superior quality over which he had little control. Was it a superior kind of love? Or was it a superior kind of power? He'd trust the love but not the power because power could parade as anything. He'd weep too, if he really believed that Moleka had a greater love than his own. What his heart said was that Moleka had a greater power than he had, and he had felt no remorse at what he had done to the only person he loved as he loved his wife. This brooding and uncertainty made him malicious. Perhaps his heart was wrong and a day would come when he would truthfully surrender his wife to Moleka, because he had decided that Moleka's love was greater than his own. If this mood was upon him, he would walk in through the door and say: 'I only married you because you were the only woman in the world who did not want to be important. But you are not at all important to me, as I sometimes say you are.'

It could turn the world to ashes. All the fire and sun disappeared because his words were inwardly lived out in his deeds. That evening, he was happy. He thought about the yellow daisies. He walked in at the door and said, softly: 'My sweetheart.'

◆

They were the most precious words, if you only knew the horror of what could pour out of the human heart; a horror that seemed most demented because the main perpetrators of it were children and you were a child yourself. Children learnt it from their parents. Their parents spat on the ground as a member of a filthy, low nation passed by. Children went a little further. They spat on you. They pinched you. They danced a wild jiggle, with the tin cans rattling: 'Bushman! Low Breed! Bastard!'

Before the white man became universally disliked for his

mental outlook, it was there. The white man found only too many people who looked *different*. That was all that outraged the receivers of his discrimination, that he applied the technique of the wild jiggling dance and the rattling tin cans to anyone who was not a white man. And if the white man thought that Asians were a low, filthy nation, Asians could still smile with relief – at least, they were not Africans. And if the white man thought Africans were a low, filthy nation, Africans in Southern Africa could still smile – at least, they were not Bushmen. They all have their monsters. You just have to look different from them, the way the facial features of a Sudra or Tamil do not resemble the facial features of a high caste Hindu, then seemingly anything can be said and done to you as your outer appearance reduces you to the status of a non-human being.

In Botswana they say: Zebras, Lions, Buffalo and Bushmen live in the Kalahari Desert. If you can catch a Zebra, you can walk up to it, forcefully open its mouth and examine its teeth. The Zebra is not supposed to mind because it is an animal. Scientists do the same to Bushmen and they are not supposed to mind, because there is no one they can still turn round to and say, 'At least I am not a ——' Of all things that are said of oppressed people, the worst things are said and done to the Bushmen. Ask the scientists. Haven't they yet written a treatise on how Bushmen are an oddity of the human race, who are half the head of a man and half the body of a donkey? Because you don't go poking around into the organs of people unless they are animals or dead.

Some time ago it might have been believed that words like 'kaffir' and 'nigger' defined a tribe. Or else how can a tribe

7

of people be called Bushmen or Masarwa? Masarwa is the equivalent of 'nigger', a term of contempt which means, obliquely, a low, filthy nation.

True enough, the woman who gave birth to a child on the outskirts of a remote village had the same thin, Masarwa stick legs and wore the same Masarwa ankle-length, loose shift dress which smelt strongly of urine and the smoke of outdoor fires. She had died during the night but the child was still alive and crying feebly when a passer-by noticed the corpse. When no one wanted to bury a dead body, they called the missionaries; not that the missionaries really liked to be involved with mankind, but they had been known to go into queer places because of their occupation. They would do that but they did not often like you to walk into their yard. They preferred to talk to you outside the fence. They had a church, a school and a hospital in the village, all founded by a series of missionaries. At that time the church and school were run by a man and his wife. There is little to say about the man because he was naturally dull and stupid, only people never noticed because he was a priest and mercifully remained silent for hours on end. He had a long, mournful face. His mouth was always wet with saliva and he frequently blinked his eyes, slowly like a cow. It was the wife who was to live forever in the memory of the child.

It is preferable to change the world on the basis of love of mankind. But if that quality be too rare, then common sense seems the next best thing. Margaret Cadmore, the wife of the missionary, had the latter virtue in over-abundance. It made her timeless, as though she could belong to any age or time, but always on the progressive side. It also made her abusive of the rest of mankind, because what is sensible is simpler than what is stupid. She had a temperament – high-strung, nervous, energetic, that made her live at the speed of a boat shooting over the rapids. Her plump cheeks were flushed by her self-imposed exertions. Continuous abuse of the rest of mankind, which moved at three quarters of her pace, had sometimes led her into situations where she was in danger of being assaulted. She had a lively sense of humour. She took revenge with a sketch pad and pencil. She gave orders and, while waiting for them to be carried out, she'd sketch the harassed face of her victim, with a note underneath for future reference, like: 'He's nice, but stupid.' It prevented her from hurling out a continuous stream of abuse.

To ensure that things happened at the speed she required, she was in the habit of getting as many people on to the job as possible. Thus, when the hospital supervisor rang up about who had died, and apologetically added that she was an untouchable to the local people, she had the coffin carried into the hospital while the grave was being dug in the churchyard. Later, when it was all over, she would conduct a one-sided, reflective monologue with her husband, George: 'I wonder where these people are buried? They don't seem to be at all a part of the life of this country.'

On this occasion her thoughts involved her. She kept her eyes screwed up reflectively as she absent-mindedly bottle-fed the baby of the dead woman. A number of things had happened all at once. Margaret Cadmore was not the kind of woman to speculate on how any artistic observation of human suffering arouses infinite compassion. She put the notes down on her sketch pad. One sketch captured the expressions of disgust on the faces of the Batswana nurses

9

as they washed the dead woman's body for burial. She scrawled a note under the sketch: 'These are not decent people.'

Her dislike of the nurses flowed out of her observation of the dead woman. As she walked into the hospital, energetically demanding the body, two nurses conducted her to a small back room where the slop pails were kept. There on the stone floor lay the dead woman, still in the loose shift dress, more soiled than ever from the birth of the child. There was horror mingled with her hysterical shouting, only she no longer cared to lecture human prejudice directly.

'Why the damn, blasted hell haven't you washed the body for burial?' she shrieked.

She was plump. Her mouth was shaped as though she was permanently laughing but she wore tinted glasses and, combined with the shouting, appeared fierce. The nurses jumped in alarm and rushed for pails and soap and water. It was only when they washed the body that they exposed their prejudice, and the reason why the body was not on a stretcher but on the stone floor. From habit she whipped out her sketch pad, then paused. The sketch would not come so rapidly. It was a mixture of peace and astonishment in the expression of the dead woman, but so abrupt that she still had her faint eyebrows raised in query. What suffering had preceded death? And what had death offered to surprise her so? She had even started to laugh.

Quite unconscious of the oddness of her behaviour, Margaret Cadmore walked to several angles of the room, studying the dead woman's expression. The note she scrawled at last said: 'She looks like a Goddess.'

She took in too much after that: the thin stick legs of

malnutrition and the hard caloused feet that had never worn shoes. She took in also the hatred of the fortunate, and that if they so hated even a dead body how much more did they hate those of this woman's tribe who were still alive. Maybe she really saw human suffering, close up, for the first time, but it frightened her into adopting that part of the woman which was still alive – her child. She had no children, but she was an educator of children. She was also a scientist in her heart with a lot of fond, pet theories, one of her favourite, sweeping theories being: environment everything; heredity nothing.

As she put the child to bed that night in her own home, her face was aglow. She had a real, living object for her experiment. Who knew what wonder would be created?

◆

There seemed to be a big hole in the child's mind between the time that she slowly became conscious of her life in the home of the missionaries and conscious of herself as a person. A big hole was there because, unlike other children, she was never able to say: 'I am this or that. My parents are this or that.' There was no one in later life who did not hesitate to tell her that she was a Bushman, mixed breed, half breed, low breed or bastard. Then they were thrown into confusion when she opened her mouth to speak. Her mind and heart were composed of a little bit of everything she had absorbed from Margaret Cadmore. It was hardly African or anything but something new and universal, a type of personality that would be unable to fit into a definition of something as narrow as tribe or race or nation. Her educator was like this. As she swore at everyone, regardless of their status, so did she tear to pieces any idea that even remotely had no grounding in good sense. And it was the simplicity of her approach and arguments that created the impression that she could open any door, make the contents within coherent, and that she stood for all that was the epitome of human freedom. Good sense and logical arguments would never be the sole solutions to the difficulties the child would later encounter, but they would create a dedicated scholar and enable the child to gain control over the only part of life that would be hers, her mind and soul. She would have to take them and apply them to the experiences gained in a hostile and cruel society. They would mean in the end that almost anything could be thrown into her mind and life and she would have the capacity, within herself, to survive both heaven and hell.

No doubt, she lived on the edge of something. The relationship between her and the woman was never that of a child and its mother. It was as though later she was a semi-servant in the house, yet at the same time treated as an equal, by being given things servants don't usually get: kisses on the cheeks and toes at bedtime, a bedtime story, long walks into the bush to observe the behaviour through binoculars of birds, and lots of reading material. Dancing through it all was a plump woman with twinkling eyes whose ideas and activities were like a permanendy bubbling stream. The child used to watch it all with serious eyes. There was nothing she could ask for, only take what was given, aware that she was there for a special purpose because now and then the woman would say: 'One day, you will help your people.' It was never said as though it were a big issue, but at the same time it created a purpose and burden in the child's mind.

It was only when she started going to the mission school that she slowly became aware that something was wrong with her relationship to the world. She was the kind of child who was slyly pinched under the seat, and next to whom no one wanted to sit.

It was odd, because she had a vantage point from which she could observe the behaviour of a persecutor. What did it really mean when another child walked up to her and, looking so angry, said: 'You are just a Bushman'? In their minds it meant so much. Half of it was that they were angry that she had the protection of a white woman who was also their principal. What was the other half? What was a Bushman supposed to do? She had no weapons of words or personality, only a permanent silence and a face which revealed no emotion, except that now and then an abrupt tear would splash down out of one eye. If a glob of spit dropped onto her arm during the playtime hour, she quietly wiped it away. If they caught her in some remote part of the school buildings during the playtime hour, they would set up the wild, jiggling dance: 'Since when did a Bushy go to school? We take him to the bush where he eat mealie pap, pap, pap.'

One day they were dancing away in savage glee, when they were pounced on by Margaret Cadmore: 'What the damn, blasted hell is going on here?' she shrieked. 'I'll have you all expelled, do you hear? I want no more of this nonsense!'

But it was Margaret Cadmore who was upset the whole afternoon. Her sharp eye had seen the one small, abrupt tear and the ugly expressions on the faces of the torturers. She liked to experiment but she dreaded drains on her emotional resources. She most probably imagined she was crying. It was only her nerves, and she was heard to mutter irrelevantly to any teacher within earshot: 'I can't understand beastliness because it would never occur to me to be beastly.'

By evening she thought she had the situation under control. That is, emotion no longer interfered with her reasoning. The only difference was that there was no bedtime story that night, no twinkling eyes, only a few solemnly spoken words: 'They are wrong. You will have to live with your appearance for the rest of your life. There is nothing you can do to change it.'

It never stopped the tin cans rattling, but it kept the victim of the tin cans sane. No one by shouting, screaming or spitting could un-Bushman her. There was only one thing left, to find out how Bushmen were going to stay alive on the earth because no one wanted them to, except perhaps as the slaves and downtrodden dogs of the Batswana. That half she would be left alone to solve. Margaret Cadmore succeeded in only half her experiment – that if an environment provided the stimulus and amenities of learning, any human mind could absorb knowledge, to the limit of its capacities. Allowance had to be made for all living beings. An allowance for life had always been made for really vicious people, who for too long had said the kind of things to helpless people which really applied to their own twisted, perverted hearts. Those who spat at what they thought was inferior were really the 'low, filthy people' of the earth, because decent people cannot behave that way.

From that eventful evening to a day seventeen years later

some wonder had indeed been created. Margaret Cadmore had produced a brilliant student, whose name, identical to hers, was always at the top of the list of passes. That the brilliance was based entirely on social isolation and lack of communication with others, except through books, was too painful for the younger Margaret ever to mention. The old white-haired lady was retiring to England. There was still one term left before her 'experiment' passed out as a fully trained primary school teacher. She came in a car with pretty floral dresses and a pair of white shoes and practical last minute advice.

'Don't wear lipstick. It won't suit you, but here's some eye make-up because you have eyes as pretty as stars. Don't forget to shave regularly under your arms and apply this perfumed powder. Don't forget to write to me.' The old plump lady pretended to cry, dabbing at dry eyes with a dry handkerchief.

One abrupt tear shot out of the young girl's eyes. The years at the teacher training college had passed by with little torture. Because of the regular appearances of the white woman and the unashamed public kisses on the cheek, she had been mistaken by the students for another variant of the word 'Bushman'. It was also a name they gave to the children of marriage between white and African. Such children bore the complexion of members of the Bushman tribe.

'Is that your relative?' they asked curiously. And she had replied, 'Yes.' There was, maybe, a little more respect granted to a half caste, but in her heart she had grown beyond any definition. She was a little bit of everything in the whole universe, because the woman who had educated her was the universe itself. There was nothing on earth that was not human, sensible and beautiful that had not been fearlessly thrown into the mind of the pupil, from Plato to W. B. Yeats. It was W. B. Yeats who had made the pupil cry. She could not grasp him.

'Damn it!' her educator had exclaimed, impatiently. 'You can't understand him because you can't hear and see the lake water lapping,' and out whipped the sketch pad. Yeats had to be there too even though he spoke of a land other than her own arid surroundings.

It was everything between them that caused a tear to shoot out of the young girl's eye. She had been more than an educator. She had been humour, laughter, fun, unpredict-able-ness, a whole life of vibrating happiness. It ended abruptly as she walked to the car. It was hard to imagine life without her. The future looked lonely.

A month later the young girl received a curious postcard from England. The ink was smudged in a number of places, as though the postcard had been posted during pouring rain, or the writer of the postcard had been crying profusely. It said, simply: 'I had to do it for the sake of your people. I did not want to leave you behind. Margaret Cadmore.'

◆

Four months later she was appointed to her first teaching post in a remote, inland village, named Dilepe. It felt like being a millionaire for the first time. She had thirty pounds, in a new handbag from her adopted mother, to ensure that she lacked nothing while awaiting her first pay cheque. The three hour journey by truck passed by in frantic, enjoyable mental shopping for all the things she would need to buy – a pot, a kettle, blankets, a plate, and other odds and ends – in the two days left free to her before the start of the first term of the school year.

It was the height of summer. There had been a little rain and the bush on either side of the road was slowly turning green. Insects had crept out of their long hibernation, and every now and then when the truck driver stopped the truck for a rest, their shrill, piercing, high-pitched wail stunned the ears. A little of that mood of summer happiness infected her heart, which was always so quiet and repressed. She had to struggle to control an urge to jump out of the truck and run away into the bush. The truck driver would surely have thought her mad. She was seated next to him in the front of the lorry and he was silent for most of the time, except to assure her that he would put her down at the school. She hesitated to tell him that it was still school holidays.

It was just past the lunch hour when they arrived at Dilepe. Fearful that the truck driver would put her down at an empty school building and she look a fool, she jumped off at his first stopping place. It was a post-office where he had mail to deliver. Directly opposite was a shop which was a combination of butcher, restaurant and greengrocer. She looked at the shop longingly. She would have liked to walk in and buy food but she had never done anything as bold in her life. She stood where she was, becoming petrified. The truck driver touched her arm and picked up her suitcase.

'Come, we'll go eat,' he said, as though aware of her lostness. 'Then I'll put you down by the school.'

There was something hilarious in his insistence that the school was her proper stopping place, and her own lack of not knowing what to do next. She followed him blindly, because he seemed quite at home and at ease in his surroundings. He took her to a partitioned-off room where there were a few tables and chairs. He made a great fuss about ordering her food, insisting that the knife and fork be carefully wiped. It was the stricken, helpless look on her face that so touched his heart.

'You must not be so afraid of the world, Mistress,' he said kindly. 'People can't harm you.'

There it shot out again, one single abrupt tear from one eye.

Was that really true? Did many people behave like him, so spontaneous in their kindness? They ate in silence. Suddenly the truck driver pricked up his ears, his face alight with interest. The tap, tap, tap of high heeled shoes approached their way. He swung around in his chair as one elegant leg swung through the partition.

'Mistress Dikeledi,' he called out loudly. 'Don't you teach at Leseding School?'

She was so startling and unexpected in her elegance that anyone could draw any number of conclusions about her and still be puzzled. The clothes were too bold, the skirt too tight but the feel of her was like a cool, lonely breeze, the kind that calms the tense, stifled air of a summer afternoon. She had a way of looking at people with one quick, wide stare, then immediately looking away into a far-off distance as though she did not particularly want anything from life or people. She had a long, thin, delicate face, with a small mouth, and when she smiled she seemed very shy.

She walked over and sat down at their table, immediately

18

lighting a cigarette with a quick, almost hidden movement of her hands.

'Hullo, Josh,' she said quietly.

She threw a quick look at the girl opposite her, then added: 'We were expecting her. Don't worry. I'll settle everything.'

The truck driver stood up and walked away. He still had many places of call. The young woman named Dikeledi looked away into the distance and spoke at the same time in that cool, assured voice: 'Would you like some tea?'

'Yes, please,' the other young woman said.

Dikeledi looked down. A slight frown flitted across her face. It was the first time the other had spoken and she could not quite place her in the scheme of things. The near perfect English accent and manners did not fit her looks. In fact, not one thing about her fitted another and she looked half like a Chinese and half like an African and half like God knows what.

'What's your name?' she asked at last.

'Margaret Cadmore,' the other said.

'Is your father a white man?' asked Dikeledi.

Since the atmosphere between them was so relaxed, the other young girl spoke without hesitation:

'No,' she said. 'Margaret Cadmore was the name of my teacher. She was a white woman from England. I am a Masarwa.'

Dikeledi drew in her breath with a sharp, hissing sound. Dilepe village was the stronghold of some of the most powerful and wealthy chiefs in the country, all of whom owned innumerable Masarwa as slaves.

19

'Don't mention this to anyone else,' she said, shock making her utter strange words. 'If you keep silent about the matter, people will simply assume you are a Coloured. I mistook you for a Coloured until you brought up the other matter.' (By 'Coloured' Dikeledi meant children of mixed marriages who also could look half Chinese, etc.)

'But I am not ashamed of being a Masarwa,' the young girl said seriously. 'Let me show you something.'

She opened her handbag and took out a small, framed picture.

'My teacher made this sketch of my mother the day she died,' she said, and handed it to Dikeledi. Dikeledi took the picture, glanced at it with that strange, wide stare, then looked away into the distance, an almost smoky haze clouding her lovely eyes.

'Did a white woman write that?' she asked. 'And about a Masarwa? "She looks like a Goddess"?'

Her face suddenly broke into a pretty, shy smile.

'I am not like you, Margaret,' she said. 'I am afraid to protest about anything because life easily overwhelms me, but you are right to tell anyone that you are a Masarwa.'

Dikeledi deliberately under-played her own achievements. She was quiet, no gongs sounded, but she was a drastic revolutionary. She was the daughter of a paramount chief and the first of that crowd to put a good education to useful purpose. They all had, and their relatives had, the best education but the best was used as an adornment of their social status. Dikeledi had no need of employment but unlike others who made wealth synonymous with idleness, wealth gave her the freedom to specialize in what interested her most. In fact, barely half a year ago she had returned from England with a diploma in early childhood education. It wasn't for her own sake either that she drew in a sharp, hissing breath.

It was an instinctive, protective gesture towards the person sitting near her. She had taken two slaves from her father's house and, without fuss or bother, paid them a regular monthly wage. They dressed well, ate well and walked about the village with a quiet air of dignity. There was something Dikeledi called sham. It made people believe they were more important than the normal image of human kind. She had grown up surrounded by sham. Perhaps it was too embarrassing to see people make fools of themselves, because at one point she said: 'I'll have none of that.' She was not alone in that decision.

She looked at her watch. It was almost three o'clock. She pushed away her tea cup and smiled: 'You have no accommodation and here we are, idling the time away.'

They stood up together. Dikeledi raised her hand.

'Wait here,' she said. 'I'll find someone to carry the suitcase to the car.'

They both thoroughly surprised each other. Margaret was amazed by her certainty that someone would carry a suitcase simply because they were asked to, as though the elegant woman was accustomed to being waited on, hand and foot. Sure enough, Dikeledi returned in a minute with an eager, obsequious man who heaved the suitcase onto his shoulder. She had not said anything about personally owning a car. She had not really said anything about herself, Margaret realized, and the neat, small, highly polished car with a pile of mail in the back seat only heightened the mystery. There was the truck driver, too, who seemed to know her well, and to whom she had spoken with such courteous, informal respect.

'She can't be what I think she is, an ordinary person like myself,' Margaret thought uneasily.

Dikeledi drove as carefully as she talked. She turned the car onto a small, dusty road that ran along the bottom of a hill.

'I'm taking you to Moleka,' Dikeledi said. 'He usually attends to the accommodation of new teachers.'

As she mentioned the name, Moleka, a happy smile lit up Dikeledi's face. She had been in love with Moleka since doomsday. There had been one quarrel in particular, but many others as well. After their quarrels he seemed quite happy if he never saw her again, but she was always restless afterwards, until some excuse presented itself for her to throw herself in his path. It was said of Moleka that he had taken his heart out of his body and hidden it in some secret place while he made love to all the women in the village. Dikeledi was the only woman who knew that. The quarrels were about where he had hidden his heart.

At the end of the road, a notice board proclaimed: 'DILEPE TRIBAL ADMINISTRATION.' There was a long row of office blocks, at the end of which was an imposing structure of modern design, painted in a contrasting range of brilliant colours. Dikeledi drove towards the brightly painted building and parked the car just outside the small gate. They kept pace, walked up a flight of stairs, then turned slightly to the left and into a long, beautifully-furnished office.

A young man sat alone. Next to him was an unoccupied chair. The young man looked up and frowned as he saw Dikeledi. There was silence. He shifted his head. He did not look at Margaret but right through her head, to the wall. There was a heavy thunder-cloud around his eyes. He looked grim and vehement and gruesomely ugly. When he spoke his voice had such projection and power that the room vibrated slightly.

'Are you the new teacher we were expecting?' he asked.

'Yes,' she said faintly.

'You've come too late,' he said. 'All the accommodation for the year has been taken up.'

He shifted his head to Dikeledi with a look that said: 'All right. Go now.' Then he looked down and continued his paper work.

There was nothing to do but go. As they walked down the stairs, Dikeledi said: 'I might have to accommodate you in my own home.' She bent her head to adjust herself to this idea. She had lived alone for some time, and liked it that way. She added: 'If Maru was here you would have found accommodation on the spot. He is almost a God in his kindness towards people, not like that swine.'

The words were hardly out of her mouth when 'the swine' appeared right behind them. He was smiling now. His teeth were enormous. He said: 'I know you like to praise me, Dikeledi.' That happy look again swept over Dikeledi's face. In her eyes there was the tenderness and devotion of a dog. She seemed to have no control over the dog love, even though the man obviously took it for granted and was flattered. He scratched his head: 'Oh, I just remembered that the old library was vacated last week and the books moved to the new library. This teacher can use it for accommodation. I'll take her right over.'

He moved quickly, took the suitcase out of the car and

transferred it to a white van, then held open the door of the van. Dikeledi said: 'I'll come in a little while to see if you are settled,' and walked over to her car.

There was something not yet said. They liked each other.

Margaret had never seen anything like it in her life. The man slammed the door shut, turned on the ignition, then there was a cloud of dust. First one goat jumped out of the road. Then six, seven or eight more. People jumped. Both people and goats looked outraged. He kept on smiling. He was royalty, the son of a chief. He'd grown up making goats and people jump. It was nothing. By the time the van swooped up a hill towards a small building she was white around the mouth from shock. It was as though there was a long trail of death behind them. As she set her feet down and looked behind, the dust of their journey still rose in the air. He seemed not to notice, having his mind fixed on his own life. He picked up the suitcase, pushed open the door and walked inside, placing the suitcase just inside the door. She followed silently. The man frightened her deeply.

It was a long single room, fifteen feet in length, with four windows. It was in good condition except that it was covered in layers of dust and cobwebs. There was only one piece of furniture, a low trestle table. Perhaps the man was retrieving his breath. He slowly paced up and down, head bent, deep in thought. She had her back to him. A big black scorpion, disturbed by their entry, scuttled with angry speed across the room, its tail alertly poised to strike. Behind her, she could hear the man walk towards the table and raise it as though to fold its supports and remove it. The day was almost over. It was too late to purchase a bed from the shop. Perhaps scorpions could not climb up tables. She swung round and burst out nervously: 'Please don't remove the table.'

He kept quite still, his hands touching the table. He did not turn round. When he spoke she could hardly recognize his voice. It had deepened in a strange way. There was something sweet in it, like a note of music, yet he only uttered one word: 'Why?'

'I am afraid of the scorpions,' she said.

He turned round slowly.

'I knew you were going to say that,' he said, as though he were talking to an old friend, whose faults and failings were quite well known to him. But there was a trick to him, some shocking, unexpected magic. A moment ago he had been a hateful, arrogant man. Now, he had another face which made him seem the most beautiful person on earth. It was only his eyes, as though a stormy sky had cleared. What was behind was a rainbow of dazzling light. Though unaware of any feeling, something inside her chest went 'bang!' Her mouth silently shaped the word: 'Oh,' and she raised her hand towards her heart.

He looked away, but when he turned his head again and looked at her there was pain and enquiry in his eyes as though he did not quite understand what had happened, as though he had been presented with something strange and unnatural which was beyond his control and he did not like it. He bent his head, trying to withdraw himself, walked slowly to the door. The scorpion crossed his path and he quietly crushed it with his foot. He paused by the door and rested one hand on the door post.

'I'll fetch you a bed,' he said, humbly.

How did life prepare one for the unusual? It only defined

what work you ought to do, what you ought to eat and when you ought to eat. But no one ever said anything about your feelings. There was a strange feeling in her towards the man, as though she were ashamed of him. She heard the van move down the hill. She laughed a little, then spoke out loud: 'But I am not that important.' He had made her feel as though she were the most important person on earth, when no one had ever really cared whether she was dead or alive, and she had been so lonely. The loneliness had disappeared like the mist before the warmth of a rising sun.

It was more than that, too. There had been no backbone to her a short while ago. Now something had stabilized her.

He seemed to have said silently: 'You see, you don't have to be afraid anymore. First there was one of you. Now there are two of you.' It was that generous.

She walked to the door. Below her the village of Dilepe spread out and swept towards the horizon. It was a network of pathways and dusty roads weaving in and out between a tortured lay-out of mud huts, as though people whimsically said: 'we want to live here', and made all the little pathways and roads follow their whims. A thousand wisps of blue smoke arose silently into the air as a thousand women prepared the evening meal beside their outdoor fires. That peace, and those darkening evening shadows were to be the rhythm of her life throughout that year, and Dilepe village was to seem the most beautiful village on earth.

She was really no longer lonely.

◆

The moon was so bright that few stars appeared in the sky. Moleka walked along the footpath, his hands in his pockets, deep in thought. He had an appointment with one of his innumerable girl friends, but being in an absent-minded mood he walked right past her hut. His thoughts so absorbed him that he even continued past the outskirts of the village and into the bush. A full yellow moon rose high into the sky. He paused at last and looked around him. Perhaps it was only this – the light in the sky and the quietly glittering beauty of the earth – which matched a portion of his body that felt like a living, pulsating sun.

Alone now, he slowly raised his hand to his heart. How was it? Something had gone 'bang!' inside his chest, and the woman had raised her hand to her heart at the same time. It was not like anything he had felt before. Dikeledi was the nearest he'd ever come to loving a woman and yet, even there, Dikeledi made his bloodstream boil by the way she wore her skirts, plainly revealing the movement of her thighs. With Dikeledi it was a matter of the bloodstream. And what was this? It was like finding inside himself a gold mine he'd not known was there before. Yet he could have sworn that he was totally unaware of the woman until she spoke. Something in the tone, those soft fluctuations of sound, the plaintive cry of one who is always faced with the hazards of life, had abruptly arrested his life. With Dikeledi it was always distractions. She was too beautiful, physically. With the woman there were no distractions at all. He had communicated directly with her heart. It was that which was a new experience and which had so unbalanced him.

He shook his head and sat on a rock.

'It's madness,' he thought. 'I hardly know her.' What were her legs like? He could not say. All the force of her life was directed to her eyes, as though that were the only living part of her. Something killed the old Moleka in a flash and out of one death arose, in a flash, a new Moleka. It was the first time he had spoken to a woman in humility, but not the first time he had felt humbled by some quality in another living being. He screwed up his eyes, puzzled. Some other person had prepared him for his encounter with the woman. There was something eluding him and he could not immediately remember the other person. There was someone like her, someone who walked into a room and made no impact but, when you turned around again, they owned your whole life.

'I have come to the end of one road,' he thought, 'and I am taking another.'

He'd lived like a spendthrift millionaire. There was something about him, or in him, that made people walk into a room and turn their heads: 'Ah, there's Moleka.' He took that physical fascination and traded it all on women. There was always enough and some to spare. Maybe he grew accustomed to having a shadow next to him.

'Moleka,' the shadow would say, shyly, 'I'd like you to introduce me to so-and-so.'

Moleka would have been just on the point of making a proposal to Miss so-and-so, but he would immediately hold out his hand.

'Of course Maru,' he'd say. 'I shall arrange everything.'

They were the words of a millionaire. There were also ramifications and ramifications. When had he and Maru not lived in each other's arms and shared everything? People said: 'Oh, Moleka and Maru always fall in love with the

28

same girl.' But they never knew that no experiences interrupted the river and permanent flow of their deep affection. It was Moleka, so involved in this river, who never had time to notice the strange and unpredictable evolution of his friend. He never knew about the gods in the heart and the gods in the earth but he could always see the light of their conversation in his friend's eyes. It was the light that Moleka was so devoted to. He never asked whether he might have a light of his own or that he might be a startling personality in his own right. His face was always turned to what he saw as the most beautiful person on earth. Thus it was that thousands of people noted the dramatic impact of Moleka, but he would always cast his eyes across the room to see if all was well with Maru.

It was only Maru who saw their relationship in its true light. They were kings of opposing kingdoms. It was Moleka's kingdom that was unfathomable, as though shut behind a heavy iron door. There had been no such door for Maru. He dwelt everywhere. He'd mix the prosaic of everyday life with the sudden beauty of a shooting star. Now and then Maru would share a little of his kingdom with a Miss so-and-so he had acquired through Moleka. But it never went far because it always turned out that Miss so-and-so had no kingdom of her own. He used to complain to Moleka that people who had nothing were savagely greedy. It was like eating endlessly. Even if they ate all your food they were still starving. They never turned into the queens and goddesses Maru walked with all his days.

Throughout this time, Moleka was the only person who was his equal. They alone loved each other, but they were opposed because they were kings. The king who had insight into everything feared the king whose door was still closed. There was no knowing what was behind the closed door of Moleka's kingdom. Maru had no key to it, but he knew of its existence because if he touched Moleka's heart with some word or gesture a cloud would lift and he would see a rainbow of dazzling light.

The clue to Moleka and Maru lay in their relationships with women. They were notorious in Dilepe village for their love affairs, and the opposing nature of their temperaments was clearly revealed in the way they conducted these affairs. The result was the same: their victims exploded like bombs, for differing reasons. At the end of a love affair, Moleka would smile in the way he smiled when he made people and goats jump out of his path, outrage in their eyes. There was nothing Moleka did not know about the female anatomy. It made him arrogant and violent. There was no woman who could resist the impact of his permanently boiling blood-stream. But he outraged them, and horrible sensations were associated with the name of Moleka. Moleka and women were like a volcanic explosion in a dark tunnel. Moleka was the only one to emerge, on each occasion, unhurt, smiling.

It was different with Maru. At the end of a love affair, a deep sorrow would fill his eyes. He often took to his bed with some indefinable ailment. The victims, too, displayed alarming symptoms. The strongest fled as though they had seen a nameless terror. The weakest went insane, and walked about the village muttering to themselves. Maru always fell in love with his women. He'd choose them with great care and patience. There was always some outstanding quality; a special tenderness in the smile, a beautiful voice or something in the eyes which suggested mystery and hidden dreams. He associated these things with the beauty in his own heart, only to find that a tender smile and a scheming mind went hand in hand, a beautiful voice turned into a dominating viper who confused the inner Maru, who was a king of heaven, with the outer Maru and his earthly position of future paramount chief of a tribe. They only saw the social gains that would accrue to them and it made their behaviour despicable to his all seeing eye. Someone always died but their deaths often turned him into an invalid. It was nothing for Maru to be laid up for three months on end over a love affair. Doctors said: 'Take those pills.' And Maru said: 'What for?' And doctors said: 'You have T.B.'

None of the victims could ever explain the process of her destruction, nor its cause. Everyone took it for granted that there was something called social position and you had to scheme and fight for it, tooth and nail. That is the world, they said, as though all the evils in human nature were there by divine order and man need make no effort to become a god. Thus, the women whom Maru made love to were highly envied. People said: 'Oh, and when is the marriage to take place?' A month or so later the girl would flee the village or become insane. A terror slowly built up around the name of Maru because of these events. In their conversations at night they discussed the impossible, that he was the reincarnation of Tladi, a monstrous ancestral African witch-doctor who had been a performer of horrific magic.

Moleka knew of all these things. They were the root cause of his violent, over-protective attitude towards Maru. It was a difficult situation. On the one hand, Maru had all the stuff that ancient kings and chiefs were made of. People had acclaimed those around on whom they could build all kinds of superstitious myths. Yet the fear and terror magicians inspired made them live with their lives in the balance. Who knew how many murder plots were constantly woven around the life of Maru? People looked to the day when he would be their chief. But a lot of people, and these included relatives, spent the days counting the nails in his coffin. He aided the counting by always taking to bed with those indefinable ailments. He had only five friends in a village of over fifty thousand people. They were Moleka, his sister Dikeledi, and three spies – Ranko, Moseka and Semana. Of the five, Moseka and Semana were shadows. From Ranko, Moleka and Dikeledi, Maru was inseparable. But it was only with Moleka that he shared all the secrets of his heart, because Moleka was a king with his own kingdom. Since no other came so close to the heart of Maru, they invented all kinds of rubbish and horrors. Moleka alone knew that all the visions and vivid imagery Maru was subjected to directed Maru's footsteps along a straight road – that of eternal, deathless, gentle goodness. Moleka walked blindly through life. He walked blindly through all kinds of sensational love affairs. The one great passion of his life was his friend, Maru.

These words were forever on the lips of Moleka as he and Maru sat together at the sunset hour, discussing the day's events:

'Nothing will ever separate us, my friend. We shall love each other, forever.'

Maru would smile quietly. One day he had a reply for Moleka. It was a message from the gods who talked to him in his heart. He said to Moleka: 'One day we will part, over a woman.'

'But that's impossible!' Moleka exclaimed.

He said that because he had never loved a woman. When he did, he wanted to kill Maru. Not even as he sat alone in the moonlit bush that night did he recall those words of Maru's. He screwed up his eyes, puzzled, as though something was eluding him. Then his mind took up the threads of his own life. He said: 'I have come to the end of one road, and I am taking another.'

He bent his head a while longer, lost in thought, then added: 'I kept my heart for her alone.'

It seemed the greatest achievement of his life. He felt reborn, a new man. No, he felt as young and innocent as a three-year-old child.

◆

It was the first day of the new school term. All the teachers who had been at the school throughout the previous year stood at the doors of their classrooms. They had already received their allocations of new pupils before the school closed for the summer holidays. The only addition to the staff, Margaret, stood near the principal's office. She looked at a group of three teachers who stood to one side, among them Dikeledi. They taught the beginners' grades. It really felt as though she could walk across to the three women, who were still waiting to have their new pupils registered in the principal's office, and feel welcome. It was Dikeledi. In the course of two days they had fallen into a relationship of wonderful harmony. There was no tension, restraint, or false barriers people usually erect towards each other. It was mostly Dikeledi. It was mostly her temperament: 'I'm all

33

right. I don't want anything from anybody.' It made you want to give her the whole world and your heart too.

The principal of the school belonged to that section of mankind which believed that a position demanded a number of exaggerated mannerisms. He kept his coat unbuttoned. He walked as if in a desperate hurry, which made his coat-tails fly out behind him. There might have been a time in his life when he had smiled naturally – say, when he was two years old. But he had a degree and a diploma and with it went an electric light smile. He switched it on and off. It was painful when he was with important people, when it remained switched on. He also behaved as though life were a permanent intrigue. Nothing could be done in a straight-forward way. He was a little like Uriah Heep, and a belly-crawler to anyone he considered more important than himself. He had to impress you with knowledge. This was as painful as his smile. His voice was heavy, determined and an authority on everything. When his face was in repose, his thick lower lip hung down on his chin.

Margaret's advance papers had aroused his curiosity considerably. Even the sight of her. He made the same error as Dikeledi, assuming she was a Coloured. That was unusual too. Such children always worked in the shops of their white fathers. He thought he'd have something to talk about, such as that she must be the first of *their* kind to teach in *their* schools. He'd also have to keep a sharp eye on racialism. Those types were well known for thinking too much about their white parent, not about their African side. He eventually approached Margaret with his electric light smile.

'Ah, Miss Cadmore,' he said.

Off went the smile, down came the lower lip. He frowned.

34

'I have decided to form an additional class outside the beginners' grade. As you know, the beginners' grade is the foundation of a child's life. I have the best teachers there, like Mistress Dikeledi. I like to have a clear conscience on the matter. I have continuously pressed the authorities, at meetings and elsewhere, to limit the number of pupils each teacher can handle in the beginners' grades so that they give of their best. Er . . .'

He paused, and looked at her closely. There was interest, curiosity there.

'Excuse the question, but are you a Coloured?' he asked.

'No,' she replied. 'I am a Masarwa.'

The shock was so great that he almost jumped into the air. Why, he'd be the sensation of the high society circle for a week! He controlled himself. He looked down. He smiled a little. Then he said: 'I see.'

The whole day he fretted. School closed just past noon. The office of the education supervisor was a stone's throw from the school. Usually they sat chatting over three or four cups of tea. Today, the list of beginners seemed endless. He kept noting out of the corner of his eye that the Masarwa (she was no longer a human being) seemed to be extraordinarily friendly with Dikeledi, who, in his eyes, was royalty of royalty. Should he warn Dikeledi that she was talking to 'it'? 'It' surely had all the appearance of a Coloured.

'There's been some chicanery,' he muttered, over and over again.

As soon as the noon bell rang he could be seen walking at a desperate pace to the office of the education supervisor. He slowed down at the door and shuffled in. The education supervisor did not go to the extremes of the principal but he was a comic too. He was a phenomenon of the African localization circuit. He was an exact replica of a colonial officer, down to the Bermuda shorts. He looked up at the principal from under his eyes.

'Seth,' the principal said. 'There's been some chicanery.

'How so?' the other queried.

'I have a Masarwa on my staff.'

The man Seth whistled softly.

'It's the Margaret Cadmore woman?' he said, looking serious. 'God, this is going to raise hell among the Totems here.'

He grabbed some files and ran his eyes down the application list. There was no requirement for a person to define his tribe or race. He looked very annoyed.

'They're going to blame me,' he said. 'I only look at qualifications. She was top of the class the whole way through. How the hell did she get *in*? God, Pete, this is a mess.'

Without seeing him, he stared at Pete, the principal. Again, he whistled softly through his teeth. Pete grinned, then he drawled:

'She can be shoved out,' he said. 'It's easy. She's a woman.'

The man Seth held up his hand.

'Wait a bit,' he said. 'I'll sound out the opinion of the Totems. Her qualifications are good. She couldn't possibly have got there on her own brains. Someone was pushing her. We don't know who and they might be important. The Totems will soon dig out the truth. They know what shoes you wore last year.'

Pete looked at him slyly. Things were not the same in

Dilepe village since the old paramount chief had died towards the end of the previous year. The Totems were all on hot bricks. A new man was to be installed some time during the year and he was an unpredictable quantity. The terror of him, too, was that he was practically unapproachable, unless he chose to make the first move. They all had to watch the pinnacle, then mouth everything the pinnacle said.

'You know they are all afraid of Maru,' Pete said 'They want to be on his safe side. They don't know which his safe side is. They don't know what he is going to do but they fear him. There's no such thing as Totems around here. There's only Maru.'

Seth just looked at him.

'Not everyone is that scared,' he said. 'I've heard from a good source that he won't make it to the day of installation. Did you hear about his latest ailment? It's diabetes.'

The conversation became side-tracked. The Totems or royalty of the village were their favourite conversation piece. Eventually one name stood out: Morafi, the younger brother of Maru.

◆

Funny how birds of a feather flock together. Pete, Seth and Morafi were always in one another's company and indeed formed a social élite of their own. The things that amused them were the kind of things that caused suffering to others. Morafi was the chief producer of the entertainment. People were inclined to protest these days when suddenly deprived of their property. Like most Totems, Morafi was a cattle thief and he had had a hey-day of thieving while his father was alive, his father being a thief as well.

Cattle thieving worked like this: it was known that the Totems owned the best bulls. Sometimes a handsome bull appeared amidst the herd of an ordinary man and he'd suddenly find himself surrounded by the vultures. Usually scouts did the dirty work. They'd say to the petrified man: 'I say, where did you get the money to buy such a bull? It can't possibly be yours. You must have stolen it from the chief.' And without further ado off they would go with the beast. How it was ever tolerated can only be explained by the terror the chiefs inspired in the hearts of the people. The terror grip was relaxing though. Too many people were becoming educated and questioning things. The men who were now in danger of losing their lives overnight were men like Morafi.

Morafi was revolting because his inborn stupidity was coupled with total insensitivity. First, he assumed that everything was all right with him because he was the son of a paramount chief. He had big, bulbous protruding eyes which were completely vacant of thought or feeling. His neck was covered in layers of fat. His stomach hung to his knees because he ate too much and drank too much. He was about seven foot tall and like Pete, the principal, he had an acquired laugh. It was staccato, squeaky – eh, eh, eh. His eyes never smiled. They were always on the alert for something to steal. He was such a shameful personality to anyone with the slightest sensitivity that perhaps the effect of him on the over-sensitive Dikeledi and Maru clarified their own destinies. He thought his little intrigues had driven them out of their father's home but they preferred to live as far away from him as possible. Of late, since he had had his father's mansion and slaves to himself, he had taken to staring at everyone with intense, screwed-up eyes: 'Do you get the message? I am terribly important.' He had also found out from the doctors that only a miracle could save Maru's life this time. He was an assiduous counter of the nails in Maru's coffin.

Morafi took Seth and Pete as the height of the intellectual hemisphere. It was his habit to condescend to discuss the important issues of the day with them. It exhilarated and uplifted him. He listened seriously as Seth explained his side of the matter that evening:

'I really don't know how it happened,' said Seth. 'I've always said: If a person's qualifications are good, that's enough for me.'

Morafi looked thoughtful.

'I really wonder what Maru is going to do about the problem of the Masarwa,' he said. 'Things are moving ahead for this country, and they are the only millstone. I don't see what we can do with people who can't think for themselves but always need others to feed them. Mind you, they seem quite contented with their low, animal lives.'

Pete also looked thoughtful.

'There's a real mystery about that one at the school,' he said. 'They don't look you in the face and say, "I am a Masarwa." It was like a slap in the face. The statement was so final, as though she did not want to be anything else. I had given her a loophole. Coloureds are just trash, but at least she could pass as one. It would have saved us an awful lot of bother.'

Pete achieved his ambition. From that evening he was a

sensation among the high society of the Totems. They all listened to him with bulging eyes. Who had ever said, 'I am a Masarwa'? It sent thrills of fear down their spines. They all owned slaves. Only two Totems were excluded from the buzz, buzz, buzz. But they heard because the whole village was alive with it by the week's end, and both Dikeledi and Moleka acted in their own ways and independently. The action of one crippled Pete, the action of the other caused a wave of shame to sweep through the hearts of ordinary people.

At that time the beginners' grade consisted of children of a varied age range. Most of the girls were six or seven, but the boys who worked as cow-herds started school from about the age of ten to fourteen. Pete coached a fourteen-year-old boy, and by early Monday morning the whole class of the Masarwa teacher was prepared for what was to take place. The only sign they gave of their preparedness was nervous giggles as they filed into the classroom. But as she closed the door and walked to the table to call the roll, a deathly silence fell upon the children. She looked up. A boy at the far end of the room had his hand raised. She knew there was something wrong. For the first week they had been restless, absent-minded. They had hardly noticed her, being involved in their adjustment to their new situation. Now they all stared at her with fascination and attention. A cold sweat broke out, down her back.

'Yes?' she asked, unsmiling.

The boy shook his head and laughed to himself. 'I am thinking about a certain matter,' he said.

Then he looked directly into her face with an insolent stare: 'Tell me,' he said. 'Since when is a Bushy a teacher?'

The room heaved a little and the whole classroom of children blanked out before her. Yet she still stood upright with wide open eyes. From a distance their voices sounded like a confused roar: 'You are a Bushman,' they chanted. 'You are a Bushman.'

It froze the whole school. There was not a teacher who did not know of the buzzing between the principal and the Totems over the weekend. They even knew what was to happen next. They waited for his drawl: 'But Miss Cadmore, why can't you control your class? You are disturbing the whole school.'

In fact, he was on cue, except that half-way across the quadrangle he saw Dikeledi streak ahead of him into the classroom of the Masarwa. He jerked himself back on one leg, looked to the left and right and started running back to his office. He still heard her voice. It was like murder, shrill and high like the shattering of thin glass against a wall: 'Stop it! Stop it! I'll smash you all to pieces! She is your teacher! She is your teacher!'

A few of the teachers in the senior classes smiled to themselves. Dikeledi had run the school for some time. She was the only person who did not understand backstabbing. They all had knives in their backs from Pete. They pulled them out that morning.

The principal sat in his office, struggling to gain a semblance of self-respect. His calculations had excluded Dikeledi. He had a pencil draft of a report on his desk: 'I find Margaret Cadmore an ineffective teacher. She is totally incapable of controlling her class . . .'

'The bossy little bitch has buggered up the works,' he muttered, over and over again.

He and his like thought only that way. They were only angry when their plans to inflict suffering went haywire. They never for one moment dreamt that their victims had passions too and that these passions were terrifying in their violence. Dikeledi was the only one among the privileged who got close enough to a traditional dog to find out the truth. She walked into Margaret's classroom during the lunch break. They had fallen into the habit of eating lunch together. She had a tin of fat cakes. Up until Margaret had brought sandwiches of Marmite, fat cakes had been her favourite food. Marmite was a new item to her, and she devoured it ravenously.

'Why did you keep quiet?' she asked pointedly.

The other young woman kept her head bent. It surprised her that they agreed about everything. She liked the fat cakes. They were made with eggs.

'I was surprised,' she replied, quietly. 'They used to do it to me when I was a child but I never felt angry. Before you came in, I thought I had a stick in my hands and was breaking their necks. I kept on thinking: How am I going to explain her death? I thought I had killed a little girl in the front desk who was laughing, because I clearly saw myself grab her and break her neck with a stick. It was only when you started shouting that I realized I was still standing behind the table. I kept saying, "Thank God, thank God! I haven't killed anyone".'

Dikeledi swung one leg on to the table.

'It's funny how we agree in feeling,' she said. 'I saw the little girl too. She put her hand to her throat when I shouted at them. I kept on looking at her because her mouth went dead white. I thought: Poor little swine. They have been

42

taught to be brave about the wrong things and laugh about the wrong things. Someone will have to teach them decency, because their parents won't.'

The door was pushed open. It was Pete. He had a little speech for Dikeledi about how she ought not to be running around the school during school hours. She flung it back in his throat with her bold, careless stare. Even his electric light smile looked sick.

'Er . . . is everything all right?' he croaked.

She kept silent. He backed out. He made another mistake, of looking into a room where the teachers of the senior classes were drinking tea together. One of them had seen him look to left and right, then dart back to his office. They now greeted him with rocking laughter. That was all. Something unhinged in him. He spent the rest of the morning talking to himself in his office. How had things backfired like this on a surefire case? What would the children say?

There was worse to come. By noon a greater sensation had swept through the village. The Totems cringed. It seemed as though the world was ending. Next to Maru, they instinctively took Moleka as the most powerful man in the village. A servant, not a Masarwa, who worked in Moleka's home spread the word that they no longer knew what was what. He said that all the Masarwa slaves in Moleka's home sat at table with him when he ate. The whole village was involved. There was no longer buzz, buzz, buzz. Something they liked as Africans to pretend themselves incapable of was being exposed to oppression and prejudice. They always knew it was there but no oppressor believes in his oppression. He always says he treats his slaves nicely. He never says that there ought not to be slaves. At this point, just past

43

noon, when everybody was saying they no longer knew what was what, Maru returned. He had been away, visiting some remote villages, to make himself, so he said, familiar with his future work as paramount chief.

◆

Ranko had the most stupid and uncomprehending face on earth. It was like rock in its total lack of expression. When people approached him or talked to him he said: 'Er? What's that?' as if he could not understand one word. So they said: 'Goodness, what a fool he is,' and left him alone. In his freedom he employed himself in the only occupation he liked. He was Maru's spy, not of any ordinary kind. Nothing ordinary was ever associated with Maru. Ranko had a camera inside his brain. It did not need to talk, only sit on the edge of any situation and take pictures, including the minutest detail. Who can explain the situation? Maru had too much intuition. He liked his inner intuitions verified. He employed Ranko to verify them. People said that Maru had second sight. He had. He could tell people what their secrets were, but he always had Ranko verify them. Ranko was like Moleka. They both wanted to protect a personality too original to survive in an unoriginal world. Their loves differed. Moleka's love was objective, ideal. As long as he held Maru up as his ideal, he loved him. Not so Ranko. The day Maru died, so would he. He had no other life.

Maru lived within the area of the offices of the Dilepe Tribal Administration. Barely three hundred yards away from his home was the home of Dikeledi. Both homes were constructed with slabs of orange sandstone, hewn from the

44

surrounding hillside. They were built at the foot of the hill, on a slight incline and long flights of highly-polished staircases led to enclosed porches where they often sat and ate their meals. The wheels of their cars had made two diverging tracks to their homes.

He glanced towards the home of his sister as he stepped out of his car. She had not yet arrived from school. He turned and ascended the staircase. So very little disturbed the peaceful serenity of his life. He was a man who talked and walked slowly, with a languid grace, loosely swinging his long arms at his side. The people who surrounded him really merged into a background where there was little noise or upheaval. He'd say to a servant: 'I'd like this,' and it would be there, but what he liked or needed was reduced to the barest minimum. It was the same with people. The majority were greeted as though they were passers-by he would never get to know. Those he wanted or loved became the slaves of an intensely concentrated affection. His was not the kind of personality to rule the masses. They knew it and disliked him for never being there on show. And yet, at the same time, he was highly popular among ordinary people. His manner towards everyone was of courteous, informal respect. Disciples like Dikeledi copied him in everything. He set the tone, seemingly, for a new world.

Ranko was already seated at the dinner table when he entered the porch. They did not bother to greet one another because their bloodstreams were one. Maru washed his hands, wiped them on a towel, then sat sideways on a chair at the table and crossed his legs. Immediately a servant appeared and placed a tray of covered dishes on the table, then walked away. Ranko did not make any move to eat.

He stared a little into the distance and quietly unrolled his camera:

'There is a little trouble in the village about a Masarwa who was appointed a teacher at Leseding school. Who knew about the Masarwa? Her certificate said: "Here is a teacher with Grade A for every subject." This news was spread by the education supervisor. Accordingly, people examined the new teacher the day she arrived. They smiled: "Why, she is a Coloured," they said. "This is most unusual. Look at the light complexion."

'The next day people noticed that the new mistress had dignity and respect for everyone. People decided to change their minds about entering their children for Maroba school. They said Leseding school was so fortunate to have so many first class teachers like Mistress Dikeledi and the new mistress with dignity. I thought to myself: "Why, there will be a commotion at Leseding school on opening day if the whole village enters its children there. Let me examine the new mistress for faults."

'I met her at the general dealer's where she was buying household goods. She picked up the parcel of household goods and walked away. Lesego, who served her said: "Hmm, hmm, you have forgotten your change." She did not hear. She continued walking, her eyes searching the ground. I said to Lesego: "Give me the change, I want an introduction. The change was two pounds. I caught up with her and said: "You are rich to throw away money, hey?" She stood still, took the change, then began to feel the parcel in her arm. Then she said: "I have lost my handbag." So I said: "The handbag is hanging on the arm which is carrying the

46

parcel. Better let me carry the parcel in case you lose the arm which is carrying the handbag and the parcel."

'I was surprised to see that she could not laugh, only cry quickly, with one eye. I thought the strange manner of crying meant "thank you", because now and then she looked at my face. Soon she became forgetful and started searching the ground with her eyes. Moleka had given her the old library room as a home but there she was, walking to Hong Kong. I said: "Where are you going?" She said: "I am going home." I said: "You are proceeding in the wrong direction." So she laughed a bit, then stopped. Then laughed again. This happened all the way up the hill to the house. I thought to myself: "She has a major fault. How can such a forgetful person teach children?"'

Ranko paused briefly. The car of Dikeledi took the track to her home. She stepped out, noted the presence of her brother, then quietly ascended her staircase. Ranko continued:

'Mistress Dikeledi was just as much head over heels in love as I was. When we came to the top of the hill she took a mat and chair from the car for the comfort of the house of the new mistress. She shouted at me: "Go away Ranko. We have secret matters to discuss and you are a spy." Then she removed the parcel from my arm by force. Since I was head over heels in love I decided to keep silent about the major fault of the new mistress, and too many people took their children to Leseding school on the opening day.

'That very afternoon people were looking at each other with shock. They said: "Did you hear? The new mistress says she is a Masarwa." By evening they began to laugh: "The eye is a deceitful thing," they said. "If a Masarwa combs his hair and wears modern dress, he looks just like a Coloured. There is no difference." Those with children at Leseding school debated the matter. They were trying to accustom their hearts to their children being taught by a Masarwa. They said: "Prejudice is like the old skin of a snake. It has to be removed bit by bit."

'Moleka, who heard that the principal and the high ups were planning trouble for the new mistress, could not make allowance for the slow removal of prejudice. He removed it all in one day. He told Seth, the education supervisor, that there was good food in his house on Sunday. When Seth arrived he found all the Masarwas in the yard of Moleka also seated at the table. Moleka took up his fork and placed a mouthful of food in the mouth of a Masarwa, then with the same fork fed himself.

'Seth removed himself from the house in great anger. He shouted for all to hear: "I shall have no further dealings with Moleka."

'Trouble broke out at Leseding school this morning. It was contained by Mistress Dikeledi. After the school closed I removed a piece of paper from the floor of the principal's office.'

He paused and handed a crumpled piece of paper to Maru. It was the partially drafted pencil report Pete had prepared. Then he continued: 'People are angered by the behaviour of Moleka. They say his action was too high handed and has created confusion. There is no place for a Masarwa, whom everyone has seen behaving like a low animal in drink and filth, and he wants to force matters and stir up trouble. From the side of the high-ups and the principal of Leseding school, matters went like this . . .'

Then he carefully reported the words and behaviour of Seth, Morafi and Pete, who thought God was on their side and had opened their mouths too wide about their prejudice. After a while there was silence between the two men, then Maru asked:

'How did Moleka become involved with the new mistress?'

Ranko replied: 'You will see for yourself that Moleka is a changed man. The day the new mistress arrived she had no bed, so Moleka loaned her a bed of the tribal property. By accident, that same evening, I saw Moleka walk far out of the village. He was searching the ground with his eyes. I thought: "What can be the matter now? Moleka is always in trouble because of his bad behaviour. But this must be very serious. Look, he passes the home of Grace, yet he was mad for her yesterday. Let me follow." When we came to the boundary of the village I had to remove my shoes because there was too much moonlight and no place to hide. I didn't want to disturb his thoughts.

'He sat down with his head bowed for a long time. Then he spoke out aloud: "I have come to the end of one road and I am taking another." A little while later he said: "I kept my heart for her alone." A little while later he stood up, still searching the ground with his eyes. Again he passed the house of Grace and went to his own home. I thought: "What's this? Moleka has not missed sleeping with a woman since the age of twelve."

'The next day I passed by the office. Usually Moleka

says: "Hey, Ranko, you damn fool, come here." That day he forgot to swear. He said: "Ranko, please fetch me a packet of cigarettes at the shop.' While attending to other matters, my heart was worried about Moleka in case he should be losing his mind. His thoughts were too deep. I did not see into his heart but there are no Masarwa slaves in his house now. Today I thought: "Perhaps the new mistress has bewitched him, the way Mistress Dikeledi and I are bewitched."'

Maru laughed a little. The cinema screen was highly entertaining to him. It seemed as though Ranko had been specially born to teach him about the oddness in the human mind and heart.

'Has Moleka made any proposals to the new mistress yet?' he asked slyly.

'No, that's gold,' replied Ranko. 'He keeps his mind on the gold mine and does not care what people think of his behaviour.'

'You know, Ranko,' Maru said, unashamed of gossiping about his best friend. 'I can't stand a man like Moleka. He has so little emotion that when he finds a speck of it he thinks it's a mountain. That's why he's troubling everyone. Also, it's not good for a man, once he has found his heart, to wear it boldly on his sleeve. He also wipes his nose there. I shall have fixed him up by five o'clock when we leave the ofiice. Please find Moseka and Semana and be here with them by that time. I am tired of those eye-sores, Morafi, Seth and Pete.'

He turned, rinsed his hands, wiped them and stood up. Outwardly he appeared calm, but something was violently agitating his heart. It was a nameless distress, of the kind when one has a premonition of bad news to come. He paused briefly at the top of the staircase and looked out on the sweeping spread of the land, sleeping in the shimmering heat of the midday summer sun. Unconsciously he spoke his thoughts out loud: 'I am lonely,' he said.

Slowly, he descended the staircase and walked to the home of his sister. She was still eating, on the porch. She looked up quietly as he seated himself. They did not greet one another. Their bloodstreams were one. He poured himself a cup of tea from the pot on the table. His sister's house had a direct view of the office where he and Moleka worked. For how long – was it years – had she sat and watched all the comings and goings of Moleka? And he had not cared.

'Ranko tells me that Moleka is trying to change the world by himself,' he said. 'Yesterday, all the Masarwa in his yard sat at table with him. He shared his plate of food and his fork with one.'

'He did?' Dikeledi said, astonished.

Suddenly Maru's heart felt light and gay. If Dikeledi did not know, who was there to tell the other woman how much Moleka loved her? His heart expanded with generous lies.

'Oh yes,' he said, smiling. 'Ranko was just explaining the matter to me. Apparently people don't like the idea of a Masarwa teaching their children. Moleka decided to teach Seth a lesson, to show him that a Masarwa is also a human being. Seth was there at lunch and saw everything. One fork of food went into the mouth of the Masarwa and the same fork went into the mouth of Moleka. I told Ranko that Moleka is a scoundrel but he has a heart of gold.'

51

So many suns lit up the face of Dikeledi and her eyes melted with tenderness.

'I agree with you, brother,' she said, almost singing the words. 'Moleka has a heart of gold.'

She sat quite still, lost in a golden glow of love, forgetting all the quarrels, the evil associated with Moleka, his arrogance. It was as though he had always had God under his skin.

'Are you going anywhere this afternoon?' her brother asked quietly.

'Oh no,' she said. 'I am up to my ears in work. I have a whole year's preparation to do in two days.'

'All right,' he said. 'I'll see you again, after five o'clock,' and he stood up. Moleka had already approached and entered the office. He wanted Moleka to be there before him, and to be seated. Who knew what would happen next? His heart was too agitated. If he had time to be alone, he knew he would be able to sort out the cause with his gods, who talked to him in his heart. But something this time was forcing him to move blindly into something. He ascended the short flight of stairs to his office, turned to the left and paused at the door.

Moleka looked up. At first Maru blinked, thinking he saw almost a replica of himself before him. The savage, arrogant Moleka was no longer there, but some other person like himself – humbled and defeated before all the beauty of the living world. So is that what love is like, he thought? And you can't hide it? Arrested, he looked a little deeper, first into Moleka's eyes, which he saw as two yellow orbs of light, and then deeper, into his heart. The humility was superficial, perhaps in keeping with his changed view of himself, but what was in Moleka's heart, now that the barriers were broken, made Maru's heart cold with fear. It was another version of arrogance and dominance, but more terrible because it was of the spirit. Moleka was a sun around which spun a billion satellites. All the sun had to do was radiate force, energy, light. Maru had no equivalent of it in his own kingdom. He had no sun like that, only an eternal and gentle interplay of shadows and light and peace.

'He is greater than I in power,' he thought, at first stunned, taken aback by the sight. Then he thought: 'How was it that nothing sealed my doors? I always knew who I was. Moleka had to wait until his door was opened by another hand. Moleka is only half a statement of his kingdom. Someone else makes up the whole. It is the person he now loves.'

He knew from his own knowledge of himself that true purpose and direction are creative. Creative imagination he had in over-abundance. Moleka had none of that ferment, only an over-abundance of power. It was as though Moleka were split in two – he had the energy but someone else had the equivalent gifts of Maru's kingdom: creative imagination. Why, any wild horse was also powerful and where did wild horses go? They jumped over cliffs. Moleka and his stupid brain could send all those billion worlds colliding into each other. Did the sun have compassion and good sense? It had only the ego of the brightest light in the heavens. Maru preferred to be the moon. Not in any way did he desire Moleka's kingdom or its dizzy, revolving energy, but somehow a life-time of loving between them was over in those few seconds. He averted his head in embarrassment and pain and quietly moved to his chair beside Moleka. There was a pile of neatly-typed mail in the outgoing tray

53

for him to sign. He had been away for three weeks and all that could be heard for some time was the scratch, scratch of his pen as he signed the letters. After a while his eye wandered to the tray marked 'Miscellaneous'. A roughly-pencilled note, in Moleka's bold scrawl, lay carelessly flung on top of a pile of papers. As his hand moved towards it, he noted out of the corner of his eye that Moleka started violently.

'What a fool he is,' he thought. 'Behaving like a sixteen-year-old girl.'

He read the note: 'Property of Dilepe Tribal Administration. 1 bed, 1 mattress, out on loan to teacher, Margaret Cadmore, assistant teacher: Leseding school.'

He turned and stared directly at Moleka's profile. Moleka kept his face shut in to himself, seemingly preoccupied with his work.

'This Margaret Cadmore must be the Masarwa who is causing trouble in the village,' Maru said.

Moleka turned round and looked Maru in the face. There was no expression or comment in his eyes.

'I don't know of any Masarwa who is a teacher,' Moleka said flatly, crying out for a showdown. He knew of Maru's spies and spies.

A glint of something dangerous, threatening, shot into Maru's eyes.

'I'm not like you, Moleka,' he said, with heavy sarcasm. 'I still own the Masarwa as slaves. All my one hundred thousand cattle and fifty cattle posts are maintained by the Masarwa. They sleep on the ground, near outdoor fires. Their only blanket is the fire. When the fire warms them on one side, they turn round and warm themselves on the other side. I have seen this with my own eyes. What will they do when they hear that a certain Masarwa in my village is treated as an equal of the Batswana and given a bed from my office? Won't they want beds too, and where do I find all those beds, overnight? I want the bed you loaned to the Masarwa teacher returned, immediately.'

He pushed the pencilled note towards Moleka. Moleka took the note, seemed to re-read it, but he was struggling to clear his head of the roar inside it. How had he and Maru become strangers and enemies, so abruptly? He jerked his face back to the face of his friend, who now had his own face shut in, seemingly preoccupied with his work.

'I'll get the bed returned,' he said, but the undertone was so violent it meant: 'I'm going to murder you.'

Moleka stood up and walked out of the ofiice. Maru raised one large hand and covered his face. He was laughing. He had a number of bombs to set off in the village of Dilepe. Some would explode soon, some a little later. This was the first time Moleka was out of it, and he was laughing because Moleka appeared just as much a fool as everyone else to his scheming and plotting. He stood up and watched from a window as Moleka gave orders to two clerks to take his white van and recover the bed. Moleka did not want to do the dirty work himself. Maru looked at his watch. The time was four o'clock.

Fifteen minutes later the white van stopped outside the solitary old library building on the small hill. Being absorbed in her notebook, Margaret did not immediately put down her pen at the van's approach. She was seated at a small table under a window and at first turned round with surprise when one of the men knocked at the open door. She stood up and walked across the almost empty room. There was little furniture. Apart from the small table and chair, there was a bed with a floor mat, a large wooden packing box, neatly covered with a clean white cloth on which was arranged a tea set, a plate, spoons, knife and fork. Next to this was a small paraffin tank stove with two plates, on one of which stood a kettle. A few books leaned against each other on the floor. Her clothes were still in the suitcase. There was an odour of freshly applied floor wax and an old wax oil cloth which covered the room from end to end sparkled in the late afternoon sun. Cheap, but very pretty floral curtains, handmade, hung at the windows. It seemed to her the most beautiful home on earth.

As she walked to the door her eye was attracted by the white van outside. For a second her heart stopped beating, then continued at an accelerated pace. She turned to the men, almost too eagerly. They just stared back at her. One of them seemed to strike her a blow in the face. He said: 'Moleka has sent us to recover the bed.'

She placed one hand on the door post to steady herself. The events of the morning rose like a wave. The abrupt demand for the bed made her mouth go dry with fear. She said: 'Oh!' It meant so much, all at once: I am going to lose my job. They are going to drive me out of the village. Why have I been thinking of him every spare moment of my life, since the day I first saw him?

'Why so suddenly?' she asked, struggling to regain her shattered equilibrium.

'He did not explain,' the older man said. 'He just told us to bring back the bed.'

Then he looked town, shame-faced, embarrassed. He was

part of the village life and knew about the mutterings concerning the Masarwa teacher. Even so, she was a teacher of their children and deserved some respect. That was his opinion. She could feel it. It gave her the kind of courage she did not normally possess. She said: 'It's a little late for me to get another bed from the shop. Could I not have a day or two to order a new one? I am sorry but I forgot to ask the secretary how long I may borrow the bed. He told me they usually lend beds to teachers.'

The two men looked at each other. They had never done anything so dreadful in their lives. The older man spoke again:

'Moleka is a reasonable man,' he said sympathetically. 'If you present your case to him, he will surely let you keep the bed for a day or two. Come, we will take you to him.'

She quickly closed the door behind her and walked with the men to the van. Oh, what, what to do? There were the children. She had not yet recovered from the shaking up of the morning. And now this! Why loan her a bed only to humiliate her with its abrupt removal? Were they all saying, like the children: 'You are a Bushman?' Perhaps she did not care about the bed. She wanted to see him again. Perhaps she would be unable to stand alone against a whole village of people who did not want a Masarwa teacher. She'd see by his face and then make her own decisions. There was a limit to which a human being could be an experiment, especially if he or she were so unprepared for something new.

The driver stopped the van outside the office. She climbed out and walked up the short flight of stairs, then turned left. She paused at the door. Two men were in the office this time. Neither looked up from his work. She stood there, trapped. Perhaps they had secretaries whom one should approach first. Just as she was about to retreat, Moleka said: 'Come in,' but his face was like stone and he did not look up. There was nothing to uphold her. Should she even try to claim that she was human?

'The request for the return of the bed is so sudden,' she said nervously. 'Could I keep it for a day or two until I buy one from the shop?'

How her whole future depended on his reply, yet his face remained stone.

'It is I who want the bed returned today,' a voice said.

She jerked her face, startled, towards the speaker. He had been outside her visual range. A look of surprise and enquiry flitted over her face. He was a replica of Dikeledi, in the delicate construction of his face, with those same far away eyes, except that his mouth was full and wide. He looked as though he was half smiling, friendly, gentle, but his words did not match his voice. That was final authority; no one could contradict.

Suddenly she felt as if her throat were being choked. The man was Dikeledi's brother. Dikeledi spoke of him with reverence. And how much had Dikeledi invaded her own life without giving her these awful details – that she, Dikeledi, was related to someone like this who had slaves as part of his hereditary privilege? Did you ever sort out one thing from another with people, especially when you were a no-people? Did you trust intuition, and if you did, how did you explain Moleka and his talking heart – first there was one of you, now there are two of you?

'I'll return the bed,' she said, and walked out as if she

were facing her death. How was she to know the true size and nature of this sudden adversary? Almost everyone grovelled before him, because of his position. But she had looked down at him, indifferently, from a great height, where she was more than his equal. It had nothing to do with the little bit of education she had acquired from a missionary. He treated everyone as a single, separate entity, and measured the length and breadth and depth and height of their inner kingdoms with one, alert glance. There was every kind of foolishness in the world. People who had nothing were as evil and malicious as Pete, and as false. People who had kingdoms were careful not to betray those gods who dwelt inside those kingdoms. How few they were. Almost everyone wrecked his nervous system like the screech of cheap music.

Some time passed and then Moleka silently left the office. It was nearing five o'clock, but Maru continued staring absent-mindedly at the wall. A picture slowly unfolded itself before him.

How often had it haunted his mind. There was a busy, roaring highway on one side, full of bustle and traffic. Leading away from it was a small, dusty footpath. It went on and on by itself into the distance.

'Take that path,' his heart said. 'You have no other choice.

Each time he hesitated. It was too lonely. No other companion trod that road. Maybe the loneliness would drive him to the busy highway, where he would meet his doom. But as he faced the choice again that late afternoon, springing upon either side of the footpath were thousands and thousands of bright yellow daisies. They stirred in the sunlight and cool breeze and turned faces of faint, enquiring surprise in his direction. Then they danced all by themselves. The sight was so beautiful that his heart leapt with joy. He stood up in a fearful hurry, like one with many preparations ahead of him. He waited for a while at his home, where he met Ranko, Moseka and Semana as arranged. Then the three men went their own ways into the village, while in the swiftly gathering darkness he walked to the home of his sister, Dikeledi. She still had her head buried in her note-book, and was filling it in with neat, rapid handwriting.

'I'll make some tea,' she said, jumping up and putting it to one side, relieved to have a genuine excuse to stop work.

He sat down and absorbed himself in his own thoughts. Soon his sister returned with the tea tray. She still held it in her hands as she talked.

'I saw my colleague enter the office not so long ago,' she said. 'It made me curious.'

'Moleka loaned her a bed,' he said. 'I made her return it.'

She put the tray down on the table so roughly that a little of the milk in the jug splashed up into her face.

'Why?' she asked sharply.

'I did it to quieten the village,' he said. 'People expect a Masarwa revolution, because of Moleka's behaviour on Sunday.'

'There's no such thing as Masarwa,' she said, a sudden shrill edge in her voice. 'There are only people.'

'Oh,' he said sarcastically. 'You think you have found a bit of humanity and can lecture to me?'

'Have you ever tried sleeping on the hard floor?' she asked, also curling her lips in sarcasm.

60

He turned his head a little and smiled. She was so confused and angry, she averted her head and picked up the sugar bowl. Nothing had to be wrong with Maru. He was her God.

'I don't like anyone to be wiser than thou about my actions,' he said, in a quietly threatening voice. 'I don't care whether she sleeps on the hard floor for the rest of her life but I am not going to marry a pampered doll.'

Dikeledi rocked backwards on her high heels, and half the sugar in the bowl reeled on to the floor. There was something like hysteria in her laughter. She thought she had everything right but suddenly an abyss opened up in front of her. She had to jerk her mind away from the words: 'But you can't marry a Masarwa. Not in your position.' How could she say that, when not so long ago she had said there was no such thing as a Masarwa?

'Why are you laughing?' he asked, sounding very angry.

'I am shocked,' she said, truthfully.

'About what?'

'Between the lunch hour and now, people don't suddenly decide they are going to marry. I think you are joking.'

'I am not,' he said.

She kept quiet for a while to control the hysteria. She put the sugar into the tea and handed him a cup, but her hands trembled and the tea cup rattled. She could not drink her tea. She was upset and distressed and burst out: 'I don't like your jokes,' she said. 'They are about a human being. If people heard even a whisper of this they would instantly plot to kill her. You know how stupid and cruel prejudice is. It can't think beyond its nose. Besides, I am involved. We

61

loved each other from the day we met. There was no difficulty about establishing the friendship. Even there I was surprised. I knew the love had to grow, gradually.'

He kept silent a while. He was almost tempted to expose Moleka and the real cause of his sudden suicide from Moleka the savage to Moleka the god. Who else made a god overnight but a goddess? If there was one thing that would kill Dikeledi, it would be to know who had found the heart of Moleka and that she had had no key to open the iron and steel doors of his kingdom. There was a world apart from petty human hatreds and petty human social codes and values where the human soul roamed free in all its splendour and glory. No barriers of race or creed or tribe hindered its activity. He had seen majestic kings of the soul, walking in the ragged clothes of filthy beggars. He could bring this home forcefully to her but the truth would destroy her and he needed her alive and stupid for his future plans. He hesitated, with pain in his eyes. Always, at a push, he told a half truth, or an outright lie. Perhaps Moleka would give her the kind of shaking up to make her rise beyond a narrow view of love.

'I hate you, Dikeledi,' he said, vehemently.

She looked surprised.

'When you think of me,' he said. 'You think of me as they all do, that I am their public property to be pushed around and directed by what they think is right and good for me. Has it not occurred to you that I might despise, even loathe them? Three quarters of the people on this continent are like Morafi, Seth and Pete – greedy, grasping, back-stabbing, a betrayal of all the good in mankind. I was not born to rule this mess. If I have a place it is to pull down the old structures and create the new. Not for me any sovereignty over my fellow men. I'd remove the blood money, the cruelty and crookery from the top, but that's all. There's a section of my life they will never claim or own.'

He could not see her face in the dim light but he saw her shake her head as though she was not following everything. In her mind he was irrevocably a paramount chief. Yes, he was good enough to be God but half the glitter and impact of him in her mind was his earthly position. Had she not time and again said to friends:

'Maru is a real chief. He is a little bit like the chiefs we had in the old days, before the white man arrived.'

How was it then that he had inherited so much blood money and so many slaves whose only blanket was an outdoor fire? Had they not all been a little like Morafi, with a few principles, and these principles had saved them from outright damnation? Maybe he concentrated on his immediate situation. It was African. It was horrible. But wherever mankind had gathered itself together in a social order, the same things were happening. There was a mass of people with no humanity to whom another mass referred: Why, they are naturally like that. They like to live in such filth. They have been doing it for centuries.

Should he bother to explain to her the language of the voices of the gods who spoke of tomorrow? That they were opening doors on all sides, for every living thing on earth, that there would be a day when everyone would be free and no one the slave of another? People no longer needed chiefs and kings and figureheads who wore dazzling garments and ruled with the philosophy that there was never enough, so those who had had to put their foot down on those who had not? New kings were arising indeed. The stature and majesty would always be there, but the kings who arose now were those of the soul who could never betray their gods of goodness, compassion, justice and truth. The downtrodden were hearing the message of their humanity. Who could contain the fury of centuries of oppression and despising? Certainly not the Morafis of the world. But people like himself, to whom a little bit of goodness was incompatible with a little bit of greed. There had to be perfection. It had to be almost ready-made, for use.

Had he not struggled with this in all his relationships with people – that goodness between friend and friend was mutual, and goodness between lover and lover also? With all his insight, he had been unable to turn a sow's ear into a silk purse. On each occasion he had simply thrown away the sow's ear and behind him was wreckage and devastation, too terrifying in its explosive vehemence. No wound had healed. He had only to touch the scars for them to bleed all over again: 'I hated her because she thought too much of herself. I hated her because she was only flesh. No flowers grew out of the love, and when I said: All right, this is over, she still thought the flesh had captivated me forever, until I had to kill her. I killed them all because of their greed.'

Should he explain every secret to Dikeledi? Maybe she would not fall in so easily with his plans. He needed a puppet of goodness and perfection to achieve certain things he felt himself incapable of achieving. He could project the kind of creative ferment that could change a world, but he was not a living dynamo. She was. So was Moleka. All he wanted was the freedom to dream the true dreams, untainted by the clamour of the world. Moleka and Dikeledi were the future kings and queens of the African continent, those of stature in character and goodness. He, Maru, was the dreamer of this future greatness. A whimsical amusement filled his voice once he began to speak again.

He said: 'Drink your tea. It is getting cold.' Then he paused, while she raised the cup to her mouth.

'I'm sorry I shocked you,' he said. 'I never intended accepting the chieftaincy. I was only born in it to see its evils and its effects on society. Everything I have done has been an experience, an experiment. I just move on to more experience, more experiment. When she walked into the office this afternoon, I merely said: That's one more experience for me, but it shows all the signs of being a good one. A woman like that would ensure that I am never tempted to make a public spectacle of myself. We'd never make the right, conventional gestures. People would never get over it, the embarrassment: "Why, she's only a Masarwa." They'd not know where to look because they spend their lives judging each other by things of no consequence.'

He began to laugh quietly. Half of him was a demon. He was only afraid of Moleka, who had his eyes and his heart and saw everything his way. Dikeledi also began laughing. His words so truly evoked the image of her new friend and certain oddities in her behaviour. If anyone approached Margaret Cadmore, she slowly raised her hand as if to ward off a blow. Sometimes she winced, but the raised hand was always there as though she expected only blows from people. There was something else funny about her. She was a shadow behind which lived another personality of great vigour and vitality. She raised her hand to hide this second image from sight, but the two constantly tripped up each other.

Dikeledi had seen that morning also that she was very violent and dominant but seemingly unable to project that hidden power. You were never sure whether she was greater than you, or inferior, because of this constant flux and interchange between her two images. It was only Dikeledi who had a permanent platform and could bound from one thing to another with little change or ill effects. Half the fascination the other woman held for her was that her breaking point could so clearly be seen – as though one part of her broke down and was mended by another, and so on. Dikeledi's affection said: 'I must take care of her.'

Dikeledi recovered her fun and bounce. She said to Maru: 'Now tell me, when is this sudden marriage to take place?'

'Oh, in my own time,' Maru said. 'I have other things to arrange first.'

'Are you going to make a formal proposal? You know, like: "I'd like to marry you, Miss Cadmore. What do you think about it?" People usually do that first in case the other party is not agreeable.'

Maru felt a little anxious all of a sudden.

'Dikeledi,' he said, sharply. 'This is a secret between you and me. As for proposals, who else do you think would want to marry her, besides myself?'

'Of course one can't say with women,' Dikeledi said. 'She could never have as many admirers as I have but I was surprised to see Ranko carrying her parcels home the other day. I thought: Where did she pick up Ranko, and so soon? Ranko had a besotted look on his face. He could not stop smiling. I had to chase him away because his behaviour was so embarrassing.'

'You must report the progress of the Ranko affair to me, Dikeledi,' he said seriously. 'Also, report the minute she mentions the name of anyone who has taken her fancy and I shall mess everything up.'

Dikeledi shook her head: 'It's a risk you are taking, brother. She might not like to marry you. We have a free world these days. People often say "no".'

'Dikeledi,' he said, deadly serious. 'If I came to you one day and said: "Look here, I have long controlled the affairs of your life. You can't even cry unless I will it. Now, if you don't agree to marry me, you will stare at the moon for the rest of your days." What would you do?'

Dikeledi put her head on one side. You went through the unbelievable with Maru. He really made people do everything he said they would, and could create such a tangle of events with his spies that it was simpler and less harassing to carry out his orders. She could not sum up the other woman. Obviously someone, perhaps the teacher she often referred to, had sheltered her from a lot of encounters with life. Dikeledi could make no secret of the fact that, in relation to men, she often suffered from high blood pressure, except that the trouble with the bloodstream had eventually boiled down to one, unattainable man.

'Women are not alike, brother,' she said. 'Of course, I'd choose you, not the moon. I'd say, "Maru is quite an ugly man but the moon is too cool for my liking." My friend is just the opposite. She is cool. You can't tell whether she can boil or not. If she can, she's not used to it because you can't see it on her face.'

He kept silent, smiling to himself. Things had always worked out that way. Moleka raised the blood pressure of even a stone, but he did other things, the way the rain made the grass and flowers bloom. When had they not worked hand in hand? They would do so again, except as enemies this time. The way he saw it, it could not be helped, but he intended coming out on top, as the winner. It was different if his motivation was entirely selfish, self-centred, but the motivation came from the gods who spoke to him in his heart. They had said: Take that road. Then they had said: Take that companion. He believed his heart and the things in it. They were his only criteria for goodness. In the end, nothing was personal to him. In the end, the subjection of his whole life to his inner gods was an intellectual process. Very little feeling was involved. His methods were cold, calculating and ruthless.

◆

It could not be imagination. He had never been inclined that way. The real, the immediate, the practical – that was his heaven and he was to resolve his destiny in one night and find himself back where he had always been, the Moleka who found it too dangerous to allow his mind to soar off the ground. What happened afterwards was a jumble of a hidden depth of music that had briefly stirred his heart and given him a strong desire for revenge. But he acted then from a safe platform, each time balancing the real, profitable and attainable against the fantasy and each time choosing the bird in the hand. Who knows what dreams could have emerged from the music in his heart had he been allowed to obtain the inspirer of the music? Because that evening he was all at sea. He seemed to have opened up a path way as yet unknown to him and just as he was about to set foot on it, with tender eyes, everything was lost. There were only doors again and what was behind them was to remain a mystery.

It must have been two weeks now, his mother calculated, that she had been afflicted with having Moleka at home. Life with Moleka was a series of high dramas, always ending in paternity cases. There were already eight motherless children living in her yard, their only justification for being there that they all looked like Moleka, with his distinctive, thundercloud brow. Her life was a continuous harassment of women, fighting over her son. It was good enough for the motherless children that she had had only one child and an enormous amount of maternal feeling. There was never any trouble with Moleka – apart from women. Yet there he was, titivating himself each evening and going out for more trouble. How long this had been going on she could not say, except that he was her son and she was used to him. There was no way in which she condemned him. She coddled and pampered him as if he were a three-year-old boy. After all, he was her only child.

Suddenly, he began behaving in an unnatural way. He was home each evening. He seemed uncertain of his next word or action and many hours passed in brooding silence. She watched with mounting anxiety, fearing that, like Ranko, he might be losing his mind. It happened that Sunday; he turned the whole house upside down by seating himself at table with the slaves of the yard. It was not that which upset his mother. Moleka had had no other com-

69

panions. He had grown up with the slaves as playmates and was just as much coddled by them as he was by her. It was the talk and confusion in the village and her clear observation of his strange behaviour at home.

But there was no woman in sight. Over the years she had put a crease in her forehead to help her pretend anxiety for all the women who fell in love with her son. Over the two weeks the crease in her forehead became very real. Frequently, during the day, she burst into tears. Just as the situation became intolerable, Moleka went out again and the next morning, as usual, there was another woman. This time she was afraid. Sparks were flying in all directions. Who would have thought a longstanding friend and relative could have caused such upheaval in the life of Moleka? She could clearly picture his face the previous evening. He'd sat for a while, on the edge of a couch in the dining room, and slowly wiped his hand across his brow, as if under great stress. When she had enquired: 'Are you not well, my child?' he had turned and looked at her with pain in his eyes. With Moleka emotion was heightened, dramatic. She could see the pain pass like continuous waves over his eyes. He kept silent. After a while he stood up and walked out of the house, forgetting to titivate himself.

That was what the sea was like. He was trying to grasp a depth of what he had lost and trying to grasp a depth of what he might gain. Why had he hesitated for two weeks? Was it because of his closeness to Maru and that they had always shared their experiences? Because he had not hidden anything until the last, fatal moments, when it was too late. Maru had surprised him by showing a side of his nature he'd never suspected was there. Look how he had spoken about owning slaves and thinking of his own comfort and pocket first. Something had fallen between them that afternoon like a deadly knife. It was incompatible with the tender, reflective mood which had enclosed his mind over the past two weeks. He had suffered under another, unfamiliar mood. He suddenly forgot everything about making approaches to a woman. He had not known what to do, what to say as a beginning and had walked round and round in circles at home. Always, something spoke to him in his heart, like deep, sweet music. He listened intently. It was a new experience for him. Previously he had only heard that such things existed, from Maru. They were stories he listened to with interest but could not comment on. They did not arouse his curiosity either. Maru always fell in love, but not he. He had sometimes seen a light like the sun shine on Maru's face. This time he felt the sun in his own heart. There was more to it as well, as though a voice moved there and spoke to him: 'But we are surely not strangers, Moleka?'

It changed too if the mover of the voice was distressed, like that evening: 'Help me. Ought I to go away? It might be that my appearance this time prevents you from recognizing me.'

That was what he struggled with. Half of him felt that he formulated those words because he was thrown off balance and at sea. He was no Maru who could ride the tides of all kinds of fancies. He doubted his heart, his mind. But distress eventually made him walk slowly out of the house.

'Perhaps I shall knock at the door and introduce myself formally: "I have just come to see if you are comfortable. If you have not enough money to purchase a bed, I can always arrange a loan." Then I shall walk away,' he thought.

But the thought of even talking to her created such a turmoil in his mind, such a roar in his heart that he stopped for a while and stared at the pitch dark night to regain his composure. As he walked along again, he analysed his feelings. His heart had grown into its own fullness, too suddenly, and he had no control over it. There was also a feeling that he constantly held his heart against hers, or his mouth against hers, and that all human language had now become superfluous and a sacrilege. With other women there was a stream of comfortable small talk, but how was he going to talk when the roar in his heart choked his throat?

'Perhaps I ought to return home and let this matter work itself out slowly,' he thought. 'I am not myself.'

In reality, he had lived many kinds of married lives. They consisted of giving orders: Do this! Don't do that! I'd like my back scrubbed this very minute. But a horror of shyness overcame him as he thought of these things in contrast with the woman who now lived in his heart. They seemed too far removed, too remote, in the same way that he had not yet had time to see if her legs pleased him or not. Then that seemed the problem to him. There was no barrier of the spirit. He had talked straight to her heart. The effect of this had been to raise almost insurmountable barriers over the physical. It was as though some other person had to find her limbs and say: All right, proceed. You may love this woman's body as well. He paused again. Again he thought: 'Perhaps I ought to return home. I am not myself.' But his feet slowly continued in the direction that led to the old library on the hill. At the foot of the hill, he paused once more and looked up. The light of a lamp shone through one of the windows. A peace settled on his heart as though the burning lamp made everything seem normal and the person within that room engaged in some activity such as eating or cooking or drinking tea. It fitted in with his idea of formality: 'I have just come to see if you are comfortable . . .'

Almost joyfully, he began to climb the hill. He had not got half way when a voice called out: 'Moleka!'

It was Ranko. He stopped and spoke in a low, deadly voice: 'What are you doing here, Ranko?'

Without any hesitation Ranko replied: 'Maru said he expected you would come this way. He asked me to give you a message. He said: "Tell Moleka to remember that he enjoys life on this earth. This is not the end for him. He will have a long life."'

There was silence. Then Moleka ground his teeth in savage fury and made an angry exclamation that sounded half like the roar of a lion.

'I would not like to be killed by a low person like you, Ranko,' he said, furiously. 'Don't you know that spying is the lowest occupation on earth?'

Ranko kept silent. Two furies raced through Moleka's heart. The words of Maru, through his mouthpiece, Ranko, were a declaration of war. He could not accept it. It meant everything was over before it had begun. And he also knew that, although he had no Ranko, he had a control over the situation. Maru acknowledged what had awakened in his heart. The woman was just as unapproachable to Maru as she was to him. He turned violently on Ranko:

'Since Maru thinks he can send messages to me, through

spies, you can also take a message to him. Tell him I say that the day he approaches her, I will burn his house down. He is lucky if I don't kill him too.'

It was only as he walked away that the shock of the abrupt encounter with Ranko gradually overcame his mind. What was this he'd seen? When had Maru had time to fall in love and move so swiftly? Look at that terrible message: 'This is not the end for him. He will have a long life.' How did a person in his right mind relate Maru's behaviour of the afternoon towards the woman with what Ranko had revealed this evening? Maru had fooled him. Again a wave of fury swept through his heart. Did it mean that a love since childhood was over in a few hours with such a betrayal?

Unconsciously his feet took him in the direction of the house of Maru. He knew his every habit, that he sometimes sat by a window for hours with his own thoughts, unless occupied with work or a guest. He was there this evening, clearly outlined by the lamplight, seated near the window, with his thoughts. Moleka stood outside, in the dark night, all kinds of murderous thoughts rushing through his mind. He did not know it but he was regaining his hold on the practical, the immediate. Here was something he could grasp at. He had been unable to grasp at his love. It had almost deranged him. For two hours he stood there but by the end of it he had brought himself fully under control. He was Moleka, but with something added.

No sooner had Maru risen to retire than he began to pity himself out there in the dark night: 'My whole life is upside down. I wander with no place to rest my head, yet he goes

74

to bed peacefully.' It still seemed to him illogical, the vileness of Maru's behaviour and his own inability to bring swift retribution on Maru. Someone had to die that night because of the fury in his heart. Maybe he'd go and find Ranko and kill him. Just as he turned, his eye fell on the home of Dikeledi. Her laughter and mockery over the years – 'don't you even dare touch my finger-nail, Moleka' – and the way she contradicted her words by thrusting her thighs in his face, suddenly gave him an outlet for his pent-up rage. Let her start that nonsense again – 'don't you dare touch my finger-nail . . .' – and he would throttle her to death on the spot.

He had not noticed for how long her house had been in darkness, but as he tapped lightly on a door which led to her bedroom it was not a second before a match went scratch-scratch and the lamp was lit. She came padding to the door on bare feet.

'Who is it?' she asked.

Moleka kept silent. She flung open the door and peered out, then drew back, startled. Moleka walked straight in through the open door to the bedroom. He sat down on the bed, then turned and stared at Dikeledi from under his thundercloud brow. She stood at the end of the room near the door, too surprised to grasp how everything had happened so suddenly. At last she said, crossly:

'What are you up to, Moleka?'

'You think I don't know about your notebook,' he said, impishly. 'Last night Moleka slept here. The other night Moleka slept there. Grace is now his latest. Well, I want to satisfy your curiosity. Tonight I'm going to sleep here.'

He bent and started to untie a shoelace.

'Moleka,' she said, frightened. 'You can't do that. Haven't we always treated each other with respect?'

'I haven't locked the door,' he said, coolly. 'Run to the home of your brother and report that I'm molesting you. He and I will settle the matter together with fists.'

She stared forlornly into the distance. It had always been like this. He said the wrong, crude things that jarred against the delicacy and beauty of her love for him. Why, she had even fallen into bed with her heart melting with love after what Maru had told her about Moleka and the slaves in his house. He was, to her, the greatest devil-may-care hero on earth. Not even Maru could compare to the dashing image of Moleka in her mind. Since she kept so silent, he paused in the act of undoing his other shoelace.

'What are you thinking about?' he asked.

'I was feeling so proud of you,' she said sadly. 'Maru told me about how you put Seth to shame on Sunday . . .'

She could not add that he rarely managed to live on the glittering peaks of his achievements. Her eyes filled with tears. He set his foot down and turned his head towards her, with glittering eyes. He could have taken his revenge that moment. There were ways of killing people without knives and guns and he had only to say: 'I did it for her, because I love her,' and Dikeledi would have been shot dead by an invisible but fatal bullet. She thought she was the queen of Moleka's heart. There was no other woman her equal in the village. She had ignored all his love affairs because she towered above every other woman of her kind, in her world, intellectually and morally. For a brief moment Moleka balanced things: 'I won't get her from Maru,' he thought.

76

'He's the devil.' Dikeledi might be his only salvation. She was, after he had glimpsed the heights of love, the next best woman on earth. He swung his whole life towards the bars of Dikeledi's prison.

'I did it for you,' he lied, slowly. 'I knew you were her friend.'

She never questioned anything. Moleka was even baffled and hurt by the one trembling hand she placed on his knee. He had hardly been aware of when and how she had moved across the floor to sit beside him. He averted his head in embarrassment. Where did a love like that come from when he had no equal to match it in his own heart? He had just begun to learn about other things, a pain of something which is earned and lost, and earned and lost again. There were things he'd do for others, never gaining any reward. There were glittering peaks of sacrifices and services given to others, but known only to him, in his own secret heart. A wry humour twitched at the corners of his mouth. He turned to Dikeledi and said in an almost conversational tone: 'I guess I've always loved you.'

She also fell in with his mood: 'I see that you are just going on undressing yourself but it is not to my liking.'

'I have no more women left, Dikeledi,' he said, comically. 'You are the last on the list.'

This did not displease her but she kept quiet, thinking about all those children born helter-skelter, here and there. So she said: 'As you know, I'm not narrow-minded about anything but I could not endure to have a fatherless child.'

Moleka gave a snort of laughter: 'Then why do you advertise your thighs?' he demanded. 'I'd like you to stop that. You think men don't know what you mean when you walk around swinging your thighs like that? They can't take their eyes off you and here you want to pretend all kinds of innocence before me. Women like you are the cause of all the trouble in the world.'

He was laughing with one side of his heart. He stood up a moment later and blew out the lamp. A wave of pain swamped him from head to toe. He had been given a blow such as he had never experienced before. He was not sure of his survival.

'Dikeledi!' he said intensely, with desperation in his voice. He meant: 'Help me! I have lost everything I ever loved.' He meant Maru. Later, although he never wanted to admit it, he had at last accidentally found a dwelling place for his restless heart. Dikeledi's kingdom was like that of the earth and its deep centre which absorbed the light and radiations of a billion suns and planets and kept on dreaming and brooding, recreating life in an eternal cycle. Moleka must have scratched his head and smiled to himself. At least he had stumbled on to something that was a true complement to his own kingdom of radiant energy. Still he felt cheated, baffled. How had one woman set his heart aflame and he had turned around and given all that fire into another woman's keeping? It was as though a prearranged trap had been set for him, as though the organizer of the trap was alertly one jump ahead of his every need. It was not at all to his liking.

Ranko, who watched over the surprising events of the night, was also rattled. He was already seated at the breakfast table, drinking his coffee, when Maru appeared. No sooner had Maru sat down than he burst out: 'Moleka is a damn nuisance! He has now taken Mistress Dikeledi as his concubine.'

Maru averted his head. He wanted to shout with laughter but that would have upset Ranko, who adored his sister. He looked at the opposite wall and said carefully: 'Don't worry about that, Ranko. Moleka will one day live down the scandal of how he made his own wife a concubine. You must pass by Moleka's home today and tell his mother that I don't approve of his treating my sister like a cheap concubine. Tell her, that when the time is ready, I shall expect her to counsel her son wisely because this is a very serious matter.'

These words relieved Ranko's troubled heart. Why, Mistress Dikeledi with her ways and education was real gold. He chuckled to himself, thinking of his encounter with Moleka on the hill, then he unrolled his camera, describing Moleka's every word and gesture in detail. Maru forgot his usual dignity and composure, threw back his head and laughed with his mouth wide open. After a while he calmed down and remarked philosophically to Ranko: 'Why must Moleka have everything? He's always touched gold and handled it carelessly. I've always touched straw. This time I'm stealing the gold because I've grown tired of the straw.'

Then he sat quietly drinking a number of cups of coffee. The sun had just begun to show its head above the hill and streaks of its early gold light splashed on to the open field in front of him. He loved this part of the day best when everything was being born anew and the air was cool and fresh on his face. His life was so rhythmical that everything seemed to happen in the same order each day, except that today his sister's car was still outside her house. She normally left before the sun could show its head above the hill, because school started early. She always walked coolly down the stairs in a neat, tight skirt with a billowing blouse, but this morning she was late and flustered and the skirt of her bright cotton frock flared out around her pretty legs as she ran down the stairs.

A lot of things had changed. He stood up a while later and walked to the office. Moleka was already in and seated. Neither greeted the other and for a while they worked in tense silence, then Moleka said: 'You are making a mistake. She belongs to me and you won't get her.'

'That's what *you* say,' Maru said, sarcastically.

'I suppose your spies have already told you that I spent the night with your sister,' Moleka said, contemptuously.

Maru kept silent.

'I'm not going to marry Dikeledi,' Moleka said, pulling down his thundercloud brow.

Again Maru kept silent.

'I hate you!' Moleka said vehemently.

'You may,' said Maru coolly. 'But don't underestimate me. I am not afraid when fighting for what is my own.'

Moleka was so angry that he picked up a pile of papers and walked into the office of the typist and began pacing up and down, not saying a word to the astonished lady. After a time the lady noticed that things were very cool between Maru and Moleka, not like the old days of roaring laughter and jokes. The news flew around the village. Maru was angry with Moleka because Moleka had taken his sister as his latest concubine. It was the kind of tangle and confusion of events Maru revelled in. Half truths, outright lies, impossible rumours and sudden, explosive events were his stock in trade. He used them as a cover up for achieving his goals. People would thwart him otherwise and he never liked to be side-tracked. He never cared about the means towards the end and who got hurt.

Even Dikeledi fell in with his games. As usual she walked into the classroom of her friend with her tin of fat cakes. At first she was distressed and uneasy to note the dark smudges of a sleepless night under her friend's eyes. Her own inner mood was one of riotous, tumultuous happiness. She put it to one side, briefly, looked very thoughtful and then said: 'I know about the bed. I don't know what got into my brother. He does not usually behave that way. In any case, we live our separate lives and don't always agree. I don't want you to be angry with me.'

Margaret kept silent and looked down.

'I have a spare bed at my home,' Dikeledi persisted. 'I can get it delivered to your home while we are still at school. You would be small-minded if you did not accept my gift.'

Margaret looked up, startled. Their friendship was too unfathomable to her, as though she could not make an effort to analyse her feelings towards Dikeledi and it would drift on and on like this, continually getting into deep water.

'I'm not small-minded,' she said, smiling.

Dikeledi immediately dived into the packet of Marmite sandwiches, sat on a desk, tilted back her head and quietly threw her thoughts into her own heart. She was thinking: 'Moleka's kisses taste like Marmite sandwiches. Moleka's kisses taste like roast beef with spicy gravy. Moleka's kisses . . .' And while she dwelt on these earthly things, a very spiritual look of divine happiness appeared on her face.

Her companion sitting opposite her, watched this pretty communication in silence. She had an unexplored gift. Half consciously, her hand moved to a sheet of paper and a pencil and, without any faltering, concentrated on capturing that lovely expression. Fifteen minutes later she put down the pencil and covered the paper with one hand. Dikeledi awoke to reality on the tail end of that secretive gesture. She sprang off the desk: 'Hey, what's that?' she said eagerly. 'Let me see it.'

She snatched up the paper. There was Dikeledi, her face uptilted, exploring heaven. She was a vain woman and highly flattered. First she said: 'I'm keeping this.' After a moment she said: 'Please take out the picture of your mother.'

She compared the two. The styles of both artists were almost identical, almost near that of a comic-strip artist in their simplicity, except that the younger disciple appeared greater than the master. It was a difference of temperament. The older Margaret Cadmore had been essentially a cold and unemotional woman, insensitive to the depths and heights of life, and the young girl high-lighted these latter qualities, at the same time emulating her skill for rapid reproduction of life, on the spot.

'Did you learn this from your teacher as well?' Dikeledi asked, shyly.

'Yes,' Margaret said.

'I like your work better,' Dikeledi, said, much put out, as though her friend had suddenly jumped up a notch or two in her estimation. She wanted to say something like: 'But your people were naturally gifted this way. There are all those rock paintings,' and the words choked in her throat.

Nothing tallied with Margaret Cadmore, whether Bushman or what, so she said: 'Your teacher must have been a good woman to share everything with you.'

'No,' Margaret said, surprised. 'She was not good. She was rich. She kept on throwing things away. I used to feel myself catching them, and that is how I learned.'

♦

Pete, the principal, was in trouble of a strange nature. Something dreadful had happened to him the previous evening to turn him overnight into a hollow-eyed, nervous wreck. The previous day had been bad enough for him. He had lost face and the teachers of the senior classes had straightened their backs. He had been unable to stop muttering to himself, even during the afternoon, and the people with whom he lodged had several times looked with appalled faces towards the closed door of his room, from which his muttering could be plainly heard. The women began whispering among themselves, doubting if they had a normal person in the house.

At sunset, he emerged dressed for an evening out. He was his own, quiet reserved self again as he shuffled out of the house. The women sighed with relief. He was a good boarder, who paid well and on time for all services. Money was not his bad point and that was all they were worried about.

Then, from about ten-thirty onwards that evening, such a terror filled their lives as they had not known in all their born days. They heard hard running footsteps, and the door was almost bashed down. They sat up in bed, frozen with terror, listening to the heavy, laboured breathing of the principal in his room. Then his muttering began again and continued throughout the long night. The man looked at his wife and his wife looked at him. The man's old mother crept into the bedroom. Their silent looks said: 'He has lost his mind.' They started shivering. He was not just anyone: he had a position. His position stifled their eagerness to shout for help.

The events leading up to this happened thus: By sunset Pete had recovered his nerve. He had formed an ultimatum which he intended presenting to Seth: 'Either the Masarwa teacher goes or I go.' That was fair enough. He could not have a repetition of the morning's events with Dikeledi getting out of control and the senior teachers laughing in his face. To his amazement, on his arrival at Seth's he found both Seth and Morafi in high spirits. He could hardly sit down before Morafi drawled: 'Well, what da ya know? Maru has shown his true colours. He walks around like a saint but touch him on his soft spot and he's just like everyone else, only worse. I'm no angel but I would not dream of taking a bed away from a woman. What da ya say, Pete?'

Pete was clearly baffled, but when he heard the full explanation his spirits soared so high that he hardly recognized himself. He was the most sensitive of the three demons and more aware than they were of a distinction between good and evil. His own actions hovered in a haze between those extremes. He could be stricken with conscience but he enjoyed double-dealing greatly. African life in a remote village afforded no other entertainment. There was only one man he had set apart from all the double-dealing: Maru. He was precious because he was socially unobtainable. The few who had stepped inside his door talked about it for weeks, then it was reduced to scandal. They only went to pry out secrets he kept hidden away. Suddenly, the god who dwelt on those lofty heights seemed very real and easily approachable to a man like Pete. In fact, he seemed another Pete. They were both reserved, with delicate mannerisms.

'I never thought Maru would do a thing like that,' he said, a mixture of joy and calculation spreading over his face.

Morafi and Seth nodded their heads wisely. They did not like to say the obvious. Maru also kept slaves and was behaving like all slave owners. But somehow the matter was now beyond their concern. There was a moment when all they could think of was the Masarwa teacher. Now she would be got rid of by Maru. They felt cleansed and uplifted, drawn together in warm fellowship for the first time. Seth was always back-biting about Pete to Morafi and Pete was always back-biting about Seth to Morafi; and Morafi jiggled the threads between the two. He often felt himself the saint because both Seth and Pete feared to back-bite about Morafi as he was a Totem. To think that they had spent even a moment's worry over the Masarwa teacher, and only to have Maru outshine them in shameful behaviour! She would not last a day longer. The whole village was behind Maru because he was already, in name, their paramount chief. They felt like saints. The devil would rule. Morafi even managed a few words of pity for the oppressed.

Just after ten o'clock, Pete left on foot for home. He walked with his hands in his pockets, a smile on his face, from the warm, glowing comradeship of the evening. A long stretch of field separated the exclusive area where the top

85

class civil servants like Seth lived, and the rambling village arrangement of mud huts where Pete lived. The night was pitch dark and he kept his face down to see the faint outline of the footpath. He had been unaware of any other person nearby. Few people moved out after sundown. Suddenly a voice quite near his ear said:

'Tladi is going to get you for your evil deeds.'

And that was all. He froze to the ground. Fright made him query: 'Who?'

'Tladi,' said the clear whisper behind his ears.

He shot his eyes this way and that. There was nothing to see. It was too dark. Besides, he had heard no footsteps. It was different if you said God and conscience. God the abstract had never lived but every African demon had once been a man with a reign of terror. Many things had distinguished Tladi from every other demon or god. He was indiscriminate about who was good and who was evil. He terrorized all. Children grew up on those tales, old people still had Tladi as a living memory. A blind horror overcame Pete. It was only the people he lodged with who heard his clamour and alarm. He heard nothing. Even in the safety of his room his alarm did not subside. It needed only such a suggestion for the whole horror of his inner nature to be exposed to him. The night was a nightmare. Every single person he had back-stabbed passed in parade before him.

By dawn he was haggard from anguish and a totally inefficient human being. As though he knew this, he did not attend school but shuffled straight to Seth's office. Unfortunately, Tladi had been busy there too. What he saw was another Pete, haggard and reduced to inefficiency like himself. They said nothing, but stared at each other with the horror of people exposed to all the torture of the demons who parade the African continent. They were intelligent. They knew it had a real, living source. Even then they could not bring themselves to utter the name: Maru. They only knew, as others before them had known, that somehow they were on his bad side and that life was not worth living if you were on the bad side of Maru. He'd terrorize you into the grave.

Three bombs went off in Dilepe village, one after the other. First, Pete the principal fled. Then Seth the education supervisor fled. Then Morafi kept looking over his shoulder for two days and he also fled. No coherent explanations were ever given, except that the people who lived with them all thought they had suddenly lost their minds. Only two men slept soundly at the end of that week. They were Moseka and Semana, who had been working overtime. Dikeledi was promoted to be the principal of Leseding School.

Part Two

The rhythm of sunrise, the rhythm of sunset, filled her life. In the distance, a village proceeded with its own life but she knew not what it was – who married, who died, who gave birth to children – nor the reason why two women on her pathway, back and forth to school, continually insulted each other in vile language for stealing each other's husbands. She was not a part of it and belonged nowhere. In fact, so quiet and insignificant were her movements that the people of Dilepe village almost forgot that there was such a thing as a Masarwa teacher. Now and then she caught their eye on her way to the shops or to school. They would laugh a bit, turn to each other and say: 'There goes the friend of Mistress Dikeledi.' She had no life outside those words.

Yet there were half suns glowing on the horizons of her heart. It was Moleka. Now and then she would pass him in the village. She could quite clearly see that he made a secret of the matter but his eyes glowed like the early morning sunrise when he glanced at her briefly. The strange thing was that the love aroused no violent emotions but blended in with the flow and rhythm of life in Dilepe. It was something to be accepted, painlessly, because there was no question of who loved whom. She thought: 'He will never approach me, because I am a Masarwa.' And it was something her whole way of life had prepared her for. Love and

89

happiness had always been a little bit far away from life as other people lived it. There could have been no better training ground than that of Margaret Cadmore, senior, whose own heart continually muddled her and who had been a woman who lived without love, without her equal in soul stature. She had missed something and was often irritable and impatient, like an unmarried woman, but the effect of it had made her draw on her own inner resources, in order to survive the ordeal of being married to a dead and stupid man.

The young girl had no confusion of heart, only the experience of being permanently unwanted by society in general. There was an inverse cycle in this. It had created in her an attraction for the unpredictable, for the types of personality most people could not abide or get along with, and for all forms of vigour and growth outside the normal patterns. Maybe she had loved a man like Moleka a thousand times, in the same odd, secret way. It did not disrupt her stability but it made the village of Dilepe hallowed ground. He fell in somewhere with those sunrises and sunsets, and the huge, spreading beauty of an old Makoba tree, just outside her window. There was a public water tap under the Makoba tree and all day barefoot women trailed up the hill to fill their water buckets and carry them home on their heads. They too fell in with the sunrise and the sunset, and her quiet dreams at night. It was like living in the shade where everything was quiet and peaceful, and she might have fallen asleep inside herself had not three companions created a hurricane of activity out of her non-working hours. One companion was Dikeledi, about whom much has already been said. The other two were a mother goat and her baby.

The encounter with the mother goat was very dramatic. She had been sitting on a rock at the foot of the hill, absent-mindedly chewing the cud in a queenly way, when their eyes met accidentally. Taking this as a suitable introduction, the goat quickly arose from the stone and followed her up the hill, the baby panting behind. She was big and snow white, the baby pitch black, with shiny, curly hair. He was barely a foot tall and about one week old. Thinking that people of the surroundings might accuse her of goat stealing, she turned round anxiously and said: 'Prr, prr, go away!' But the goat only stared back astonished, slightly insolent: 'I know my way around here. Are you so sassy as not to want visitors?'

She led the way up the slope with animated footsteps. The child cried: 'Mme, mme, don't walk so fast. I can't keep up with you.' His mother paid no heed. She was intent on making a breakthrough. It wasn't every day that there was an opportunity to collect gossip. She was old as goats go and age brought wisdom and boldness. She quivered from head to tail as Margaret put the key in the door, then, not awaiting an invitation, she stepped high and mighty into the house. She threw her revolving, ancient, hooded yellow eyes around the room and said: 'Ah! So that's what it's like inside?' Then she shot a wicked look at Margaret and added: 'My curiosity will get me killed one of these days, but I can't control it.'

The child had by this time caught up with his active mother. He dived for the udder. The journey up the hill in

91

the broiling midday heat had made him so thirsty that he made loud, snuffling noises as he gulped down his drink. His little back part stuck up in the air and he frisked his tail like a windscreen-wiper. Goats, like people, know whom they can take advantage of and, as far as the mother goat and her child were concerned, they had arrived, to stay. The ageing queen slowly made her way to a position near the door. A touch of arthritis had set in. She creaked down carefully, placing a portion of her head and nose in the sunlight, which streamed in through the door, and immediately started to doze.

Not so the little one. He performed a few delicate acrobatics and waltzes all by himself across the floor. A moment later he stopped and made a puddle, and on to it added a few neat pills. Then he was off again, then puddling. Life was too good to him. He radiated joy. The owner of the room watched in fascination as she sat down to a lunch of tea and bread with some stew left over from the previous evening. So intrigued was she by the antics of the glowing little goat that she still had her plate in her hand an hour later when Dikeledi's car stoppd outside. Dikeledi burst in in a flurry of excitement, then stopped, appalled. The puddles and pills were all over the floor and the acrobatics were going on and on.

'Get these beasts out of here!' she shouted. 'Come on! Prr! Prr! Outside, you damn nuisance! Outside, you damn pests!'

This was just what the old queen wanted. She rose quickly, on stiff forelegs, raised the hair on the back of her neck and, lowering her head, charged at Dikeledi. Dikeledi fled screaming across the room: 'God, help me! The beast is not normal.'

Alarmed at the sudden roar of laughter inside her, Margaret slid off the bed and half pushed her head under it. She stuffed a portion of her skirt into her mouth, to stifle her laughter. Dignity and Dikdedi were the same names and only a day or so ago she had become principal of a school, too.

'Margaret!' Dikeledi screamed, trapped in a corner. 'What are you doing? Help me. The beast is going to kill me. It's got rabies.'

'I'm looking for a shoe to hit the goat,' a stifled voice said, but it only moved deeper under the bed.

Seeing that she had the situation under control to her satisfaction, the queen slowly moved back to her position at the door. The child had watched all, with wonder in his eyes. He hopped, leapt and skipped over the floor for another drink. Margaret crept out from under the bed. She carefully avoided looking at Dikeledi.

'I wonder what's going on here,' Dikeledi said, regaining her composure.

'She did the same to me,' Margaret said. 'I can't chase her.'

'I suppose she thinks she's the Queen of Sheba,' Dikeledi said, looking scornfully at the goat.

A roar of laughter came from Margaret. Dikeledi, who thought her name for the goat highly inventive, laughed too. She stepped daintily around the puddles and pills and seated herself on the chair near the bed.

'I came to ask you something,' she said smiling. 'Please make another picture of me. I lost the one you made the other day.'

It was a lie. She had taken the sketch home and shown it

to Maru. He had taken it and put it in his pocket as if it were his rightful possession. Not any amount of pleading would make him give it back. All he said was: 'She will make lots more for you.'

Why, she had not thought of that. A gold mine was a gold mine. Its production ought not to stop with one dig. She thought she ought to set her face in a pretty pose and be patient while Margaret set her plate down and looked around for paper and pencil. But her own heart was laden with sorrow. She was not confiding by nature. She kept her affairs to herself. They were the more terrible to endure because of this. Moleka had gone on his rounds again, most probably with that cheap girl, Grace. She had no way of undoing her love for Moleka. It seemed a burden she would carry for the rest of her life because her heart remained stubbornly fixed on him as though no other man in the world existed. A mournful expression filled her face and she slumped a little in the chair, depressed. Sometimes, she smiled through the tears which dripped on to her lap.

The other, uninvolved person watched this alertly and captured that mingling of smiles and tears. The little puddles and pills on the floor dried up. The Queen of Sheba and the Windscreen-wiper dozed in the slanting rays of the afternoon sunlight. In the silence it seemed an hour had passed. At last Dikeledi arose. She hardly glanced at the sketch in her hand. She did not say goodbye. She walked thoughtfully to the car and drove away. Not long after that the Queen of Sheba and the Windscreen-wiper took their way down the hill. She stood at the door of the old library and watched their homeward journey until they were lost in the maze and tangle of pathways and mud huts. As always, a thousand wisps of smoke arose from a thousand out-door fires as a thousand women began to prepare a thousand evening meals. The peaked caps of the mud huts stood out in sharp, black relief against the darkening sky.

'Why did she cry?' Margaret wondered, uneasily.

Her own heart was so peaceful. She stood where she was, empty-handed, but something down there belonged to her in a way that triumphed over all barriers. Maybe it was not even love as people usually think of it. Maybe it was everything else; necessity, recognition, courage, friendship and strength. There was nothing to grasp then, or cry out for. It was continuous, like the endless stretch of earth and sky, and if she never knew anything other than his name, the feeling was greater and more generous than life, as though her heart said: 'Wait and that will grow in its own time. Wait and you will grow in your own time, but slowly, like eternity.' It freed her to work and live with vigour.

She turned indoors and slowly swept up the pills of the Windscreen-wiper. Then she closed the door, lit the lamp, set the kettle on the stove, sat down and stared deep into her own, peaceful heart.

◆

The schools had closed for the holidays that morning at the end of the first term. Fifteen days of leisure were ahead, except for Dikeledi who had to depart that afternoon for a conference of principals of primary schools in a village two hundred miles away from Dilepe. Knowing this, Margaret was surprised when her car stopped outside the old library. She had been busy waxing the old oil cloth but she quickly arose to her feet and walked to the door. Dikeledi had an enormous parcel in her arms and was smiling mysteriously. She walked straight in and placed it on the bed. The outer wrapping had already been removed and its contents examined.

'Hurry up and have a look,' she said impatiently. 'I have to go.'

Margaret lifted the lid, then abruptly sat down on the bed to steady herself. Inside was an assortment of every kind of material an artist could need – oils, water colours, charcoal blocks, drawing ink, paper and brushes.

'Did you buy these?' she asked, stunned.

Dikeledi averted her head. They had been ordered by Maru.

'Yes,' she lied.

'They're very expensive,' Margaret faltered.

'Don't worry about that,' Dikeledi said. 'I want the pictures.

She looked sharply at Margaret. She had a message to deliver: 'You must experiment with everything in that box, see,' she said, like one talking to a little child. Margaret looked up quickly, with the gesture and sudden turn of the head of a very young child with its first toy. That was the last link she had with coherent, human communication. How did Dikeledi leave the room and when did she leave? She could not say. Life was totally disrupted and another rhythm replaced it which made day and night merge into a restless fever. It had a beginning like the slow build-up of a powerful machine but once it had started the pitch and tautness of its energy allowed for no relaxation; the images and forms, the flow and movement of their life imposed themselves with such demanding ruthlessness that there was no escape from the tremendous pressure. It was as though, subconsciously, everything had been arranged especially for that time and for those days when it did not matter if she could not eat for two or three days, or if she ate at four o'clock in the morning. There was a part of her mind that had saturated itself with things of such startling beauty and they pressed, in determined panorama, to take on living form..

Somewhere, in the blur, the little Windscreen-wiper kept on dancing and snuffling down his milk and the Queen of Sheba walked the earth with majestic calm. At some stage her hands trembled uncontrollably and she stood up to make tea or wash with a fierceness quite out of proportion to those simple, ordinary activities. It was like all those other agonies of life which she had endured in silence, only those agonies had been linked with everyday things. Now she had lost the link completely, like a non-swimmer suddenly thrown into deep water. She could not discipline and control the power machine of production.

Dikeledi did not see those two days of total collapse and breakdown because by the time she came back it was all over. She only picked up, joyfully, the end product, those sheets and sheets of paper which exploded with vigour and movement. Everything else looked the same, the old oilcloth glittered in the afternoon sun and the kettle boiled on the stove. Her friend still moved around in her quiet, insignificant way. The big, dark patches under her eyes from all those sleepless nights and foodless days were rapidly receding. But Sheba and the Windscreen-wiper had taken the full blast of it. They had been stared at with savage intensity.

They had been subjected to sudden, blinding blows if they thought a certain object on paper was edible and had been astonished, when a plateful of food that was not shrubs or husks, had been thrust under their noses, yet they would not give up their regular, routine, daily visits, not for anything in the world.

'How did you do all this work?' Dikeledi gasped, carefully piling the thirty sheets of seemingly neat, detached activity on top of one another.

Margaret turned round and smiled. There was no word to explain the torture of those days, but out of it she had learned. Something inside her was more powerful than her body could endure. It had to be brought under control, put on a leash and then be allowed to live in a manageable form. She would never do work like that again. Everything else would be at a slower, studied pace.

'I had a holiday,' she said simply.

Dikeledi shook her head.

'I am ashamed to steal all these pictures,' she said. 'But I have to. They are so beautiful.'

'You may take them all,' Margaret said, knowing she was a millionaire.

As Dikeledi gathered the sheets together, she separated three of them. They were not of Dilepe village, the Queen of Sheba, or of herself. A theme ran through them. There was a pulsating glow of yellow light dominating pitch black objects.

'What's this?' she asked.

Margaret put down the teapot and walked over to where Dikeledi was seated on the bed. She hesitated when she noticed which three pictures Dikeledi had set to one side.

And yet, Dikeledi accepted anything; there was no blockage in their communication.

'I had a strange experience,' she said slowly. 'Each time I closed my eyes those pictures used to fill all the space inside my head. One picture was of a house. Everything around it and the house itself was black, but out of the windows shone a queer light. It did not look like lamplight and it revolved gently. While I concentrated on this picture, it slowly faded and another took its place. There was a wide open sky and field. I saw the pitch black clouds envelop the sky, but when I looked at my feet the whole field was filled with yellow daisies. They stirred a little as though they were dancing. Their movement also created this effect of gently revolving light. The next moment I was surprised to find myself walking along a footpath between the lovely daisies. I looked up again and a little way ahead I saw two people embrace each other. I stared quite hard because they were difficult to see. Their forms were black like the house and the sky but, again, they were surrounded by this yellow light. I felt so ashamed, thinking I had come upon a secret which ought not to be disclosed, that I turned and tried to run away. Just then a strong wind arose and began to blow me in the direction of the embracing couple. I was terrified. They did not want anyone near them and I could feel it. I dropped to the ground and tried to grab hold of the daisies to save myself from the strong wind. At that moment I opened my eyes. The funny thing was, this happened again and again until I put the pictures down on paper.'

She had separated the scenes into three. The house stood alone with its glowing windows; the field of daisies and the lowering sky made their own statement; and, on their own, two dark forms embraced in a blaze of light. Dikeledi picked up the last picture. The outline was very clear, even though the faces and arms and bodies were blacked out. She followed the silhouette of the taller person with her eye, then raised her hand to her mouth to stifle an exclamation of surprise. It was unmistakeably that of her brother, Maru. She turned an uneasy glance on Margaret, who stared back at her quietly with no change of expression.

'You frighten me,' she said, her eyes wide and startled.

'Why?' Margaret asked, surprised.

'Do you always see things like that?' Dikeledi asked.

'Yes,' she said. 'I drew all the pictures from pictures from my mind. I first see something as it looks but it looks better when it reappears again as a picture in my mind. The only difference with those three pictures was that they were new. I had not seen them before.'

Dikeledi picked up the pictures in her arms. She was feeling agitated. Margaret raised her hand a little: 'Wait,' she said. 'I am pouring the tea.'

'Hmmm?' Dikeledi said, absent-mindedly.

'Have some tea,' Margaret said.

'No,' Dikeledi said. 'Not now.'

She looked into her own heart and walked out, deep in thought. Life appeared to be a mystery, a deep interwoven tangle. She had had a glimpse of something new and altogether outside her usual speculations. How had he done it? How had he projected his dreams on someone so far removed from him? That sort of thing was meat and drink to Maru but it changed the picture when some other living being was on the receiving end of his dreams, especially such a true and sensitive recorder as Margaret. There were many

100

things she doubted about Maru. He was too rich in speculation and mystery. But Margaret? Everything about her was direct, purposeful and straightforward.

'Why,' Dikeledi thought. 'She has changed my life. I am becoming a more sincere person.'

She stopped the car outside her brother's house, picked up the paintings and walked up the long flight of stairs. He was sitting on the porch, drinking tea. She placed the pile on his knee.

'Here is your payment, you rogue and thief,' she said. 'How do you think I feel, always stealing for you?'

Without a word, he straightaway separated from the rest the three pictures.

'What did she say about these?' he asked.

'Oh, those are only dreams,' Dikeledi said, in a deliberately careless voice.

'I was waiting for them,' he said quietly.

He raised his head a little and stared into the future, with great joy in his eyes. Dikeledi, in turn, stared at him, enraptured. At times he could look a very beautiful man. His eyes seemed to say: Oh! . . . I am going to be so happy.

'I want my pictures,' she said softly.

'You will get them when I have no more need of them,' he said.

◆

He had the pictures neatly mounted on a long board and placed against the wall of the room where he sat alone with his thoughts. They were a companionship between the present and the time when he was ready to live a different

101

life. On the surface, he lived much the same life, that of a pampered person who had never lacked anything, but in an undercover way he made feverish preparations for a freedom and life wherein everything he owned would be his, not other people's blood money and stolen goods.

'We suppose you will accept the chieftaincy quite soon?' the elders of the tribe questioned him.

'Not yet,' he said. 'My health is not so good.'

And they went away, shaking their heads sympathetically. Nothing could change the fact that he was born their king, even if he was a strange one who delayed accepting the crown. Moleka, who watched his every move with suspicion, could betray him to no one. Before Dikeledi he kept silent about his heart, his thought being that she was the bird in the hand, while birds in the bush were too difficult to obtain. Besides, Dikeledi's house was a good look-out point on the actions of his one-time friend. It was his intention to expose Maru to the whole village should he ever dare to take as his concubine that silent, isolated person on the old library hill. Moleka was sure he was after something like that, and it gave him a savage pleasure to note that Maru could find no opening anywhere. He also kept the fire boiling between them with many subtle threats. Dikeledi, who could have enlightened him on her brother's secrets, was now totally absorbed in her own painful love affair with Moleka. She had questioned Maru on the fact that he and Moleka appeared enemies. Maru said it was over Moleka taking her as just another one of his string of concubines.

'Surely that's my affair,' she had replied, haughtily.

'Not entirely,' he said sorrowfully, because he was

stricken with guilt at having made Dikeledi the pivot of his plans. In another way, he was in the same position as she was, waiting to acquire a love that he, like Dikeledi, felt ought to be his.

It was more painful for him because he had to make bold moves on very intangible substance. He'd stare wistfully at those three beautiful pictures of the house, the field of daisies, and the dream of a great love, and question himself: 'If we have the same dreams, perhaps that means something.' In the end, he sent Moseka and Semana to a place many miles from Dilepe to prepare that house, and to Ranko he would confide this and confide that when they sat in the room where he kept the pictures.

'She's a great woman, don't you think, Ranko,' he'd say eagerly. 'Who can paint pictures like that?'

'Oh yes,' Ranko would say and slap his hand on his knee and roar with laughter. He had never seen anything like the actions and acrobatics of the little Windscreen-wiper. Sometimes he seemed about to walk right out of the paper, licking his tiny pink tongue, he was so alive and busy.

Maru took in the whole range and depth of the pictures. It was as though he had fallen upon a kind of music that would never grow stale on the ear but would add continually to the awakening perfection in his own heart. She chose her themes from ordinary, common happenings in the village as though those themes were the best expression of her own vitality. The women carried water buckets up and down the hill but the eye was thrown, almost by force, towards the powerful curve of a leg muscle, resilience in the back and neck, and the animated expressions and gestures of the water-carriers as they stopped to gossip. They carried a message to his own heart: Look! Don't you see! We are the

people who have the strength to build a new world And his
heart agreed. Dikeledi with her delicate expressions and
coddled life, was given the same treatment, until she too
belonged amidst the vigour of the goats and water-carriers.
What she was trying to give birth to had carved wounds
around her mouth and eyes. Even the happy pictures –
Moleka was here last night – had a guarded, cautious,
reserved look in the eyes and out of them a third Dikeledi
was emerging, who sat alone and aloof and stared with
deep, penetrating eyes on the value of her own kingdom. It
was as though, once she knew everything and had uncovered
her own worth, she would awaken and share her gifts with
those who needed them. The portraits and sketches traced
this unfolding of the soul.

He wished he could leave the matter with the remark he
had made to Ranko, that the creator of all this vitality was
simply a great woman in herself, with no other attachments
or identification. Being so highly individualistic himself, he
dreaded working out any conclusions along those of tribe or
race. But the conditions which surrounded him at the time
forced him to think of her as a symbol of her tribe and
through her he sought to gain an understanding of the
eventual liberation of an oppressed people. There was this
striking vitality and vigour in her work and yet, for who
knew how long, people like her had lived faceless, voiceless,
almost nameless in the country. That they had a life or soul
to project had never been considered. At first they had been
a conquered tribe, but the conquered were often absorbed
through marriage. Who could absorb the Masarwa, who
hardly looked African, but Chinese?

How universal was the language of oppression! They had said of the Masarwa what every white man had said of every black man: 'They can't think for themselves. They don't know anything.' The matter never rested there. The stronger man caught hold of the weaker man and made a circus animal out of him, reducing him to the state of misery and subjection and non-humanity. The combinations were the same, first conquest, then abhorrence at the looks of the conquered and, from there onwards, all forms of horror and evil practices. The Batswana thought they were safer than the white man. He had already awoken to the fact that mistreated people are also furious people who could tear him to shreds. They were still laughing with such horror in their midst, finding it more inconceivable than the white man to consider the Masarwa a human being. Thus the message of the pictures went even deeper to his heart: 'You see, it is I and my tribe who possess the true vitality of this country. You lost it when you sat down and let us clean your floors and rear your children and cattle. Now we want to be free of you and be busy with our own affairs.'

At this point in his thinking a great agony would fill his heart and he would walk over to Dikeledi.

'Ask your friend if she would like to marry a Masarwa,' he'd say.

Dikeledi would bring back the reply: 'She says she does not know.'

That was why he dreaded any tribal or racial identification. You could not marry a tribe or race; at least he could not. Such things interfered with the activities of his gods who bade him do things outside any narrow enclosure or social order.

He liked his own dreams and visions. They created an atmosphere where not only he but all humanity could evolve. They stretched across every barrier and taboo and lovingly embraced the impossible. There was no such thing as a slave or any man as an object of pity. But while he looked ahead to such a world, he was no fool. The vicious, the selfish, the cruel – those too he saw, and their capacity for creating misery. Where he could, he nailed them to the ground, but always alertly with no intention of becoming their victim. And he intended following his own heart without in any way becoming the victim of a stupid, senseless, cruel society into which he had been born. Hence his lies and evasions.

The battle between Moleka and him was one of visionaries, but he had trained Moleka to look at life with a visionary eye. Why then should Moleka assume superiority over the master? They kept their horns locked like that: 'You won't get her. And you won't get her.' But Moleka was at a dead end, powerless to make a move either way, powerless to make his love evolve beyond a glance. He, Maru, had his spies running up and down, smoothing the way for his future. He did not rest either, but began secretly and quietly to undo the ties of his birth. As for his love, it could grow and grow beyond the skies or the universe. It knew no barriers. Now and then, he could do with a little confirmation of his dreams, as when Dikeledi had brought him the pictures.

All these dreams and thoughts took place in moments of optimism which alternated with periods of great despair. Arrogance was a show with him, to frighten people. He was very humble.

At such times he would think: 'What will I do if she does not love me as much as love her?' A terrible reply came from his heart: 'Kill her.'

◆

Dikeledi supplied the easel and board; also the huge square of off-white canvas cloth, which together they stretched tightly and pinned to the edges at the back of the board. There were other tender little gestures. She had collected a number of lids of old tins and, afternoon after afternoon, she sat on the floor patiently blending different shades of oil paint into a texture which resembled the natural colouring of the earth of Dilepe at the sunset hour.

The Queen of Sheba and the Windscreen-wiper had started having trouble with their diet. The summer was over and every shred of grass had disappeared from the ground. From a miller in the village, Dikeledi had purchased a bag of husks for Sheba and her baby and they continued to swell with fat and happiness while the other village goats were reduced to lean skeletons, eating bits of dried, wind-blown paper in their desperation. The funny thing was that the owners of Sheba and the Windscreen-wiper never seemed to bother about their comings or goings or how they spent their days or what they ate. They lived somewhere in the maze of huts and dutifully returned home each evening. They were a source of many jokes between the two friends.

'I have a funny feeling about Sheba,' Dikeledi would often observe. 'I think she is a human being in disguise. Have you heard about the witches in this country? They can turn themselves into lions and buffalo. Sheba was once a witch who was starving and turned herself into a goat. She behaves just like a beggar who is also a blackmailer.'

Of course Sheba would pretend great indifference to these remarks but her child would listen very alertly, then in goat language say: 'It's true. It's true. My mother is a witch. Look at how black I am,' and he would take a great leap through the legs of the easel. They were indeed becoming very superior goats. The Windscreen-wiper had learned the ways of civilized human behaviour and now made his puddles and dropped his pills outside.

The days were so happy they seemed to speed by on wings. The same things were done each afternoon and the picture of Dilepe, at the sunset hour, slowly unfolded on the canvas. Dikeledi only became more pensive and silent towards the latter part of the year, while her friend Margaret grew in strength of purpose and personality. Perhaps constant communication and affection assisted the subconscious change in the way Dikeledi became more like Margaret and Margaret more like Dikeledi, or perhaps it was Dikeledi's love which brought to the forefront the hidden and more powerful woman who dwelt behind the insignificant shadow. The slowly unfolding landscape was very much part of this emerging personality who had lived with and loved someone in silence for a long while.

'I am composing this for Moleka,' she told herself, well knowing that the day would never arrive when she would be able to approach him with a gift or thank him for removing the loneliness from her heart. It was never only the sun which went down over Dilepe but his shadow behind the sun and the memory of her first evening in the village when she had stood alone in the dusty room and laughed a bit and felt the most important person on earth. Then she had denied it: 'But I am not that important', and those spontaneous words had echoed through the events and solitude of the subsequent months. Each day, at sunset, she walked to the door and looked out at the whimsical arrangement of huts and pathways, the darkening shadows and the whispers of blue smoke in the still air. They made her heart say other, spontaneous things; that this peace and flow and continuity was only a brief resting place, that one day she would have to say goodbye to him, that there was an accident in the whole arrangement and he had only been a kind passer-by who had given a helping hand to a lost soul. It was as though she had put out her hand and said: 'No, no, don't go so soon. I can't manage without you. I need someone to lean on.' Because he still stood there, at the door, in that arrested, humble pose and she stood, the days through, quietly leaning on his shoulder.

In the end, she began to compose that scene. Its contours began from the slope of her hillside, encircled the village and swept towards the horizon where a half-sun gazed with a glowing eye into her heart. Only the two people who stood at the doorway with their still, unchanging love remained forever anonymous.

Dikeledi caught the mood of her purpose and the depth of peace and eternity which built up in the work. It was at odds with her own painful, restless heart which had love one day and lost it the next. She would intrude now and then with her anguish.

'I wish I was like you, Margaret,' she said, wistfully. 'You look as though you could live like this forever. You look as though you don't want anyone or anything except this library, the painting you are doing now and your school work. I feel so restless. Sometimes I could just rush out of this village, forever.'

Margaret turned around and looked at her, quietly. They did not know how near they were to killing each other. One of them was the top dog, just then, silently and secretly drawing on all the resources of the sun. The other knew she lacked something. It was there one day, gone the next. They had only to mention his name and one of them would die. Margaret, who was in the more powerful position at that time, compressed her lips. Any other woman would have said: 'I am peaceful because Moleka loves me.' But then she was not any other woman. She was a Masarwa. She thought Dikeledi would reply: 'Don't be silly. Moleka can't possibly love you. You are a Masarwa and he's . . .'

So she said what she thought Dikeledi would like to hear: 'I am peaceful because I have nothing and I want nothing.

It was reasonable, even if not truthful. Dikeledi had several times asked her if she would like to marry a Masarwa, as though a Masarwa was a special freak in Dikeledi's mind. Dikeledi's mysterious smiles quite escaped her.

'You might say so,' Dikeledi replied, smiling as though she were hiding something behind her back. 'You might think you have nothing, but to my way of seeing things you are quite a beautiful woman. You will be surprised at whom you will marry one day.'

She was to remember those words one day when certain events occurred to throw her from the quiet, static niche she had found for herself. That peace was only for one year. It was to depart forever after that. She was to become another

110

Dikeledi who alternated happiness with misery, finding herself tossed about this way and that on permanently restless seas. She would have preferred that static, endless hour which moved neither forward nor backward. Fate carried out another destiny through which, by force, she had to move onward and onward, uncertain, ill at ease. There must have been a premonition. She recorded the hour of peace.

◆

The events, when they occurred, went off, one after the other, like bombs. They were well-timed, too. There were two more days left before the close of the school year and the beginning of the long summer holidays. On the second last day, Margaret put the last touches on the canvas of Dilepe at the sunset hour. The tip of the tail of the Windscreen-wiper had not yet dried when Dikeledi burst excitedly into the room. In fact, she had been in an up-and-down state for the past week, distracted, absent-minded, wistful and sometimes hysterical. Once she said abruptly to Margaret: 'I'm going to get married,' but did not stand still long enough to explain whom she was to marry. The whole village knew and was still buzzing over the commotion. They were openly saying that the marriage was a forced one, and eyeing Dikeledi's thickening waistline. There had been whispers from Moleka's mother about how she had been terrorized into forcing the issue and everyone was going buzz, buzz, buzz, especially as Dikeledi was getting fat in the wrong places. Dikeledi picked up the snickering and giggles behind her back and spent a great deal of her time crying in her house. Since Margaret was the only one outside the village gossip whose attitude and affection remained unchanged. Dikeledi couldn't bear to mention the whole sorry affair until the last possible moment. Even on that day she only remained long enough to remove the canvas, hardly glancing at Margaret's forlorn face, which clearly said: 'I want it for myself. It is the only record I have of something which profoundly affected my life.'

She stood alone in the room, feeling drained and exhausted. For a whole year her life had been this room and the paintings. It had been a most terrible discipline but the reward had been the production of that canvas. And then again, it felt as if a cycle had completed itself and that what was behind was done with, was finished.

'Maybe she was right to take it away,' she thought. 'I only seem to say goodbye to everything.'

How was she to know that Moleka would receive her gift after all, in an unexpected way, and that the message of its stillness and peace would reach his heart and that he would know he was as powerful and continuous as the earth and the sky? It would set him free and give him the space and time to attend first to affairs at hand. In this strange tangle of secret events, secretly they all assisted each other. When Dikeledi tentatively offered the canvas to Maru, he stared at it coldly for some time and said: 'No, you keep it. I don't like it.'

'But it's very beautiful,' Dikeledi protested. 'It's her best work.'

'It's not for me,' he said.

His expressionless face told her nothing, but as time went by she was to be surprised at the adoration and attention

Moleka lavished on the picture. It was to seem as though he came home each night specially to look at it, then wash and eat. It was to become an immovable part of their life together.

Of all this, Margaret knew nothing. Only, that evening as she walked to the door the magic of the sunset hour was gone. Maybe it was because the rains were so late that year and the hot earth was baked to powder by the sun. The shimmering dust of the day became mingled with the irritated wisps of smoke from the fires, as though the women who cooked outdoors were harassed and bothered by the heat and dryness and kept on disturbing the fire. Something was over and lost. A great unease filled her heart. She looked for a prop, for anything to help her recapture those lovely hours. But not even the Queen of Sheba and the Windscreen-wiper were there to walk down the hill in the late sunlight. They had not appeared as usual that day. The unease turned to foreboding. She closed the door, walked to the stove and put on the kettle. Even those usual gestures were of no avail. The peace in her heart had flown away.

By morning, after a restless night, she had made up her mind to leave Dilepe for a short while, if only to take a short train journey to another village or area. It was the last day of school. There was nothing to do. Even the promotions of the children had been completed on the previous day. From many classrooms came singing as the children grouped themselves together to entertain one another with concerts. Dikeledi came and joined Margaret's class with that of another teacher for a concert. Then she rejoined Margaret in her classroom. Her eyes were red with weeping.

'I wanted to talk to you,' she said.

Then there was a long silence, before she said: 'You will come to the wedding tomorrow afternoon?'

'Yes,' Margaret said, surprised, not knowing that the marriage was to take place so soon.

'Tell me,' Dikeledi said. 'Would you marry someone only because you were going to have a child?'

Margaret hesitated and shifted uncomfortably. They had never had personal discussions before and she knew nothing about Dikeledi's private life, except that now and then she attended parties where she made rude and hilarious comments about the high society of Dilepe.

'It would depend on the man,' Margaret said tentatively.

'That's the trouble,' Dikeledi said, nodding her head. 'All I know is that I love him. He tells me he loves me but you don't know where you are with Moleka . . .'

She saw Dikeledi's mouth move a while longer, but no sound reached her. A few vital threads of her life had snapped behind her neck and it felt as though she were shrivelling to death, from head to toe. The pain was so intense that she had to bite on her mouth to prevent herself from crying out loud. Oh, what did all the reasoning help now? There was a point at which she was no longer a Masarwa but the equal in quality and stature of the woman who sat opposite her. It was their equality which had given Dikeledi the unconscious power to knock her down with a sledge-hammer blow. No other woman could have killed her, but she knew Dikeledi through and through and her soul was a towering giant. She tried to raise her half-broken neck, to say some word that would be a remembrance or even a coherent recollection of the affection they had lived with for a year, but her throat was a tightly constricted knot of pain. She pathetically balanced the still unbroken part of her neck in the palm of her hand.

All this passed unnoticed by Dikeledi. She was swamped by her own sea of troubles, but still alive, still swimming. She had no idea that a near corpse sat opposite her. After a while she looked at her watch. It was ten thirty. She stood up restlessly and said: 'I'm going to dismiss the children.'

Somewhere, vaguely in the distance, the bell rang. Then a roar rose from over two thousand voices as the children fled in all directions for the beginning of their holidays. There were a few scattered murmurs of voices. Dikeledi walked to her car, and departed. Then silence.

Margaret got up carefully, on shaking legs. Everything was unbalanced and broken. She slowly reeled homewards but it was no longer the earth and sky; only a still, cold, dead world with no sun. By the time she reached the bottom of the hill, she drew in her breath with painful gasps. There was at least some place to hide, and she crawled determinedly forward. Half-way up the hill, a woman carrying a water bucket on her head turned to her anxiously and asked: 'What is it? What is the matter?' She tottered past, breathing painfully, without replying. The woman stared after her, open-mouthed.

Outside the door, in a blinding daze of pain, she saw the little Windscreen-wiper, alone. He was trembling from head to toe in an agony all his own. The previous day he had seen his mother slaughtered before his eyes. It had almost deranged his mind. His owners had tied him to a tree and that morning he had broken free of the string and run away. He darted into the safety of the room. She pushed the door shut. The remaining threads went snap, snap, snap behind

115

her neck and she half-stumbled, half reeled to the bed and fell on it in a dead faint.

The water-carrier spread the news among her friends: 'The mistress who lives on the hill is so sick, she is dying.' This was soon picked up by Ranko, who ran in alarm to Maru.

'Is she sick, Ranko?' he said smiling. 'Is she dying? Don't worry about that. Let her suffer a bit. It will teach her to appreciate other things.'

◆

In spite of their gossip, the whole village turned up at the wedding party. The invited guests were inside Dikeledi's home. The uninvited spread themselves out in the field and revelled in a continuous flow of home-brewed beer and slices of meat roasted on the coals of an outdoor fire. Indoors the invited guests behaved no better and as late afternoon wore on they became very drunk until little discrimination was left between who was invited and who was uninvited. Everyone mingled happily. It only mattered that the beer did not end.

Three people alone remained sober. Dikeledi anxiously watched over the hostility of the two men. She knew well enough that Maru had forcefully engineered the marriage and Moleka's eyes said all kinds of things of a highly dangerous nature to him across the room. She noted that if Maru moved here, Moleka would soon follow. He never took his eyes off Maru. Frequently, Dikeledi ran into the bathroom and burst into floods of years. A murder was surely going to take place between Moleka and her brother.

She could not know that Maru was silently enjoying himself. He had his own programme well-timed. He had also arranged that the beer should flow like an unending river and, hearing this, it was not long before every inhabitant of Dilepe was drawn to the area. It was a wedding to end all weddings.

At about seven o'clock it was pitch dark, and Maru approached Dikeledi and said he was going home as he was tired. Moleka saw him moving towards the door and roughly caught Dikeledi by the arm: 'Where is he going?' he asked suspiciously.

'He is going home,' she said, bursting uncontrollably into tears.

Moleka walked on to the porch. By the torches of firelight in the field, he saw Maru ascend the stairs. Shortly after, he lit the lamp in the front room, moved about a little, and seated himself, as a dim shadow, behind the thick curtains. Moleka went indoors. He began to relax; he was fond of beer. He drank two pints, went on the porch and noted that Maru still sat at the window. He stopped long enough to pass a curse on Maru: 'You will sit like that for the rest of your days but you will never approach her,' and went indoors for more beer.

Just as Moleka uttered the curse, Ranko slowly turned the van up the slope of the hill which led to the old library building. Inside were Maru, Moseka and Semana. The van stopped. Maru flicked on the torch and walked to the door, followed by his comrades. The whole village was still, the roar of its life being concentrated at the home of Dikeledi far in the distance. Not even the flickering torches of firelight could be discerned. The door was unlocked. Maru pushed it

117

open and walked straight to the bed. She still wore her clothes of the previous day and had not moved her position. Her eyes were wide open. They did not flicker as he flashed the torchlight into her face. It frightened Ranko out of his mind and he burst out: 'I told you she would be dead by today.'

'She's not dead, Ranko,' Maru said gently. 'It's only her neck that's broken.'

A flicker of surprise moved over the still face on the bed. It was true. How did he know? Who was he? She frowned, struggling to assemble her shattered mind. Maru watched intently, then turned to Ranko: 'You see? Get busy and put these things into the van. See you leave nothing behind. I'll fix her up.'

Of course, Ranko made a great show of minding his own business but he pricked up his ears and listened to everything as he helped Moseka and Semana remove the small pieces of furniture to the van. As he listened to the persuasive voice now gentle and understanding, next moment impatient – his heart expanded with devotion. Maru could talk a donkey into growing horns.

'You think my neck was not broken a thousand times over like that because you did not love me,' he said softly. 'It's not an ailment you die of. Sometimes you recover in a moment, especially when the cause of it is a worthless man like Moleka. You think I don't know everything? Moleka did not want to approach you because he is such a tribalist. I watched everything, thinking you might see that I loved you too. Dikeledi gave me all your pictures, except the last one.'

He could quite clearly see the movement of her eyes in the dark and that she had begun listening intently, with surprise.

'I can show you the house you painted some time ago,' he said. 'Would you like to see it?'

Since she kept silent, he became impatient: 'Self pity is something I don't like. Other people have suffered more than you. You must stop this self pity. There's nothing hurting you any more.'

His words were true. She had been so cut off, so choked, so throttled that quietly the smell of the earth began to seep into her nostrils again and even the saliva started to flow in her dry mouth. She moved her limbs and they tingled painfully from idleness but the blood in them began to flow. What kept her silent was this stunning event. She could make nothing of it. Perhaps she was dreaming. She struggled to an upright posture, but even to regain her life and movement again was a joy in itself. She had been incapable of movement or thought or feeling for hours and hours and hours and a portion of her mind which was still alive felt it keenly as the past year had been the most vital and vivid of her life. She was to question that sudden breakdown, that sudden death later, but what filled her now was this slow inpouring of life again.

'Where are you taking my things?' she asked, and the tight knot of pain no longer constricted her throat.

Before he could reply, Ranko, at the far end of the room, dropped the torch on the ground with a loud crash. He had been making a last minute check to see if any item, other than the bed, had been left behind. His flash-light had disturbed the sleeping Windscreen-wiper, who made a loud

119

grunt. Ranko, his nerves stretched to breaking point over Maru's affairs, sped across the room.

'There's a strange animal here, Maru,' he said.

'Ranko, you are a fine spy. Go back and kill that lion,' said Maru, enjoying himself.

He could feel the bed shaking, as though she was trying to suppress her laughter. She said: 'It's the goat.'

The Windscreen-wiper padded softly across the floor. He was captured by Ranko and began to yell about murder. Once Ranko had solved that, he stood by the side of the van scratching his head. There was a great deal of silence from the inside of the room. He feared to enquire because he did not like to disturb Maru when he was concentrating. Perhaps he was arranging his marriage. If so, it took quite some time and the three men watched the constellations shift their positions in the sky.

'All right. We can go now,' he said, startling them out of their reflections.

Then Maru too turned and looked at the sky, while his friends collected the last object in the house. What would the future be like? He couldn't tell, but at that moment he felt as if he had inherited the universe. He turned to the woman standing silently beside him, and said: 'We used to dream the same dreams. That was how I knew you would love me in the end.'

What could she say, except that at that moment she would have chosen anything as an alternative to the living death into which she had so unexpectedly fallen? He was not just anything but some kind of strange, sweet music you could hear over and over again. She was beginning to listen. It was not strange. She had heard it before.

As she climbed into the van, the Windscreen-wiper was on the front seat making stifled noises from his trussed-up mouth. She debated with herself a moment. He was not her goat, but she kept silent and decided to steal him. Ranko turned the van slowly down the hill, wound it through the maze of pathways and on to the highroad that led out of Dilepe. They were heading straight for a home, a thousand miles away where he sun rose, new and new and new each day.

◆

It was just after midnight when Dikeledi gave him the note. It was from Maru, who had instructed her to give the note to Moleka at that hour. It said: 'Moleka, by the time you read this I shall be many miles away from Dilepe. I am marrying too, almost at the same time. Remember that people quarrel but they should always make it up again. Maru.'

Moleka walked out on to the porch and looked across at the house where a lamp still burned in the front room and a dummy sat by the window. He began to laugh and thought: 'So he has fooled me once again. I knew I'd never get her from him. He's the devil!' And he laughed and laughed.

Everything else went smoothly for Dikeledi after that. She found she had a real husband who had begun to tire of people making a noise in his house. She watched in admiration as he began to give orders left and right. As he closed the door he turned to Dikeledi and said:

'Did you know that Maru had planned to run off with the Masarwa school teacher?'

121

'Oh no,' she said innocently.

'I was very surprised to read about it in the note,' he said.

◆

When people of Dilepe village heard about the marriage of Maru, they began to talk about him as if he had died. A Dilepe diseased prostitute explained their attitude: 'Fancy,' she said. 'He has married a Masarwa. They have no standards.'

By standards, she meant that Maru would have been better off had he married her. She knew how to serve rich clients their tea, on a snowy-white table cloth, and she knew how to dress in the height of fashion. A lot of people were like her. They knew nothing about the standards of the soul, and since Maru only lived by those standards they had never been able to make a place for him in their society. They thought he was dead and would trouble them no more. How were they to know that many people shared Maru's overall ideals, that this was not the end of him, but a beginning?

When people of the Masarwa tribe heard about Maru's marriage to one of their own, a door silently opened on the small, dark airless room in which their souls had been shut for a long time. The wind of freedom, which was blowing throughout the world for all people, turned and flowed into the room. As they breathed in the fresh, clear air their humanity awakened. They examined their condition. There was the fetid air, the excreta and the horror of being an oddity of the human race, with half the head of a man and half the body of a donkey. They laughed in an embarrassed way, scratching their heads. How had they fallen into this condition when, indeed, they were as human as everyone else? They started to run out into the sunlight, then they turned and looked at the dark, small room. They said: 'We are not going back there.'

People like the Batswana, who did not know that the wind of freedom had also reached people of the Masarwa tribe, were in for an unpleasant surprise because it would be no longer possible to treat Masarwa people in an inhuman way without getting killed yourself.